'I can sleep with the kn
away from my bed, however n

'Just out of curiosity,' Jace queried, puzzled, dubious and distinctly probing. 'What in the hell are you waiting for?'

'I don't know what you mean,' Tammy answered evasively.

'Try again,' Jace smiled wickedly, stifling a yawn.

'I haven't met the right man.'

'Do you think you've met the right man now?'

'I'm still searching,' Tammy answered, not daring to look at him.

'I see.' Jace's amused eyes flickered. 'So I'm not in the running then?'

Tammy busied herself with smoothing the duvet on the spare bed, her heart beginning to pound loudly against her ribcage. 'These are fresh sheets, so you should sleep comfortably,' she steered.

'I'd sleep better next to you,' Jace coaxed.

'I don't think I like being equated with a sleeping pill.'

'Who's talking about sleeping?' Jace remarked. 'You can *put* me to sleep.'

SONIA SEERANI

brings the afrocentric lifestyle and world of love together in this novel of passionate contemporary romance for you, a woman of culture.

A characteristic writer, she has been the published author of two children's books and reports, 'I don't even recall how I started writing, I was so young.'

WHAT IS PEACOCK AMOUR?

Peacock Amour is an exciting new line of contemporary romances which features all the elements of the modern cultural lifestyle interwined into sensual, provocative and thrilling stories.

Our goal is to give you, the reader, what your heart desires, allowing you to experience all the excitement, passion and joy of falling in love with the positive images you really dream about.

We will always try to give you stories you will remember in novels you'll treasure forever.

FANTASY IS GOOD, BUT SEX IS REAL

The writer and publisher of Peacock Amour would like to emphasise that this novel is a work of fiction. When practising sex, be safe. Always use a condom. If in doubt, consult your family practitioner.

Protect Your Life

A new romance for today's woman of culture

Significant Other

SONIA SEERANI

For Parissa

PEACOCK AMOUR

The Peacock is the only bird species that radiates the
beauty of colour. Like the woman of culture, it glows
at its best only when its attraction turns to love.

PEACOCK AMOUR and the Peacock device are trademarks of The Peacock Publishing Company.

First published in Great Britain 1993 by The Peacock Publishing Company P O Box 438 SHEFFIELD S1 4YX ENGLAND

British Library Cataloguing in Publication Data
A catalogue record for this book is available from the British Library

Copyright © Sonia Seerani 1993
ISBN 1 898441 00 6
Printed and bound in The Channel Islands

CHAPTER ONE

'EHEY BABY,' the West-Indian man drawled sluggishly. 'What a party!' He had a twisted smile and Tammy Caswell wondered without particular interest who he was. A friend of Calvin's probably, she thought with a level of disgust. Certainly not the calibre of a possible client.

'I wouldn't know,' she responded, adopting a shallow smile as she tried to push past him and enter the plush London penthouse apartment. She was late. The taxi hadn't arrived on time, but then again, she hadn't really wanted to come. Calvin, as usual, insisted that she be there. He had a knack of doing that - tactfully reminding her of her obligations to the company and to their ageing grandmother who had founded and built the firm before successfully floating it, in part, on the stock market.

The night pace just wasn't her scene anymore and that surprised her. After all, wasn't she the girl who always enjoyed life to the fullest? A Caswell. Young, single and the only female executive, second to her grandmother, on the board of Europe's most rated afro-cosmetics company.

'What you name?' the man slurred, offering her a lazy wink as he seized her wrist, his face oddly possessive.

'Miss Caswell,' Tammy answered, keeping her voice calm and inoffensive. The last time she had been invited to co-host one of Calvin's client hunting publicity parties, a semi-drunken pass by a Rastafarian was met with a deliberate brush-off and a cheeky enforced slap about the face. She was later to find out when confronted on the matter by an angry Calvin that the man had been a renowned businessman who owned a large chain of Afro-

European beauty and hair salons and Caswell Cosmetics had lost a well sought contract to supply them. Since then, she'd decided to handle any fresh propositioning with an air of cool, fiesty indifference.

'Eh eh,' his grip slackened. 'But kiss me neck back. Another Caswell?'

'I beg your pardon?'

'Me a dead fe see what a going to go on here,' the man grew excited. 'Your brother just leave after one almighty showdown with . . .'

'With me.' The stranger who arrived at the door was definitely not a party guest. Instinct told Tammy that. His cool brown eyes surveyed her from top to bottom with the same scrutiny of a sculptor; his firm-lipped mouth, bleeding on one side, was nevertheless pursed into a hard line and his expression blazed with such dark forbidding contempt that Tammy's razor sharp mind considered seeking refuge immediately.

His jaw was sporting evidence of one of Calvin's accurate left-right hooks. What had actually taken place she didn't dare guess, but it had obviously delighted their semi-drunken guest. 'Have we met?' she asked drily.

'Not officially,' the stranger answered, smoothing his shirt collar beneath his suede tailored jacket. 'And I sincerely hope you are not about to display the same impeccable bad behaviour I have already had to take from that hot-headed brother of yours whose only intelligence seems to lie in practising amateur boxing.'

'Excuse me?'

'I have, for some hours, been trying to contact at least one of you. I expect you both imagine the company to operate by itself.'

Tammy raised her eyebrows. For a strikingly handsome man in his mid-thirties, his conduct was extremely rude. 'I don't see the company to be any of your concern.'

'Tell me,' the stranger boomed, wiping his mouth with a clean handkerchief, cold eyes appraising every detail of her

'I - I don't know what you mean.'

Jace strided the floor toward her. 'Do I have to spell it out for you?' he said tightly.

'I . . .' Tammy gasped as Jace's hands slid beneath her jacket and instantly cupped the roundness of her breasts, his thumbs locating the hardened peaks of her nipples.

'You know you want me,' he told her hoarsely, holding her tightly against him and making her blatantly aware of his thrusting manhood pressing against her. 'And that's how much I want you, so don't imagine that you're going to hold out against me forever, because I won't let you. Not whilst we're married.'

Tammy tried to wrench herself free. 'You're coldblooded and coldhearted,' she gritted, trying to ignore the delicious brush of his wet bare chest against her cheek.

Jace's grip tightened as he looked down at the delicate young beauty in his arms. 'If I've given you that impression, then I think it's time we used that bed,' he blazed, 'but of course you didn't come here for that. So just why are you here?'

'I came to talk to you,' Tammy blurted. 'I just wanted you to know that I'd lied about Jason Lee. I never really encouraged him and I happen to think it totally ridiculous that you should even concern yourself over something that happened two years ago. I haven't plagued you about your past relationships, so why . . .'

'Because I know Jason Lee,' Jace interrupted jealously. 'I've met the man. I've seen what a slimeball he is and I ask myself how on earth you could even look at that jerk let alone kiss him.'

'I just don't know what the hell to say to you,' Tammy chided. 'Jason Lee is a fine looking man in his own right, but not all men can be Mr Supercool as you've obviously considered yourself.'

Jace's grip slackened. 'I see.'

Seeing the rage momentarily fade in his eyes, Tammy added, 'And for all intents and purposes, I *am* still a virgin.

You may believe that or not if you wish. Nobody's taken that away from you. Now may I please go?'

'You know,' Jace began abruptly, his expression stolid as he harshly released her. 'I kept telling myself that it wouldn't work out between us, that we were too much at odds with each other. But the more I thought about you, the more I knew I'd never get over you.'

'Then why are you treating me like this?' Tammy asked softly.

'If you must have the truth dammit, I want you, very much, but I'll not force you to love me. Now go if you must.'

Jace's admission was said so relunctantly and with so much dislike that it was several seconds before his words actually sunk in. When they did, life bloomed into Tammy's face at the realisation that Jace wanted her to love him.

With her voice dazed as much as her mind, she whispered, 'I love you.' There. She'd said it. She'd opened herself to him to accept or reject whichever he chose.

The relief Jace experienced was such that he wasn't sure how to cope with it. Tammy was in love with him, his mind whirled, his eyes searching her face, appreciating the unconscious pose and pride in every graceful line of her body. She was wise, stubborn, wilful, courageously defiant, sexy and blatantly provocative and he loved her. He drew a laboured breath before he asked, 'Say that again.'

'I love you,' Tammy repeated hoarsely, her senses instantly jarred by a deep emotion that suddenly stirred erotically inside her. 'And you can make me stay if you want to. That's why you booked this suite isn't it? I have to admit, I'm quite surprised.'

A shattering feeling of tenderness made Jace's hands reach out and cup Tammy's face between his palm, his fingers trembling over her smooth features. She was looking at him with unconcealed surrender, love glowing in her eyes so intense, he felt both humbled and sensually aroused.

'Tammy,' he said with a deep, raw ache in his voice, his body already responding to the rampaging demands his own emotions were having on his very soul. 'I love you too.'

He saw the tears of joyous disbelief filling her eyes and immediately crushed Tammy against his pounding heart, kissing her forehead, her cheeks, her earlobes and then finally her lips. 'We'll have a blessing on July 5th,' he whispered urgently against her earlobes. 'That should satisfy our social obligations and . . .'

'Sssh. Don't say anything,' Tammy whispered against Jace's lips, arching her body deliberately against his rigidly aroused frame. 'Just put us both out of our misery.'

Jace needed no more urging. Tammy felt herself caught up in his arms, feeling as though her whole body had been touched by magic as her hunger matched Jace's in a violent storm of passion.

He slowly unbuttoned her jacket and then quickly assaulted the zip on her skirt and as both items fell discarded to the floor with the remnants of loose confetti, Tammy began to feel an excitement engulf her like a chaotic whirlwind. Jace's hands swept across her smooth walnut brown body to unhook her bra and within seconds he'd removed the object. Then he moved lower, down to the silky smoothness of her thighs where he attacked the lace of her panties, along with the blue garter which prompted a delicious chuckle within them both.

A shudder rippled along Tammy's nerves at the first brush of Jace's lips. She heard her name whispered softly against her cheeks moments before his mouth came back to hers. He opened them hungrily with his tongue and began to lick playfully against her lips until she was totally tormented with desire.

Tammy began to wonder how many more unfamiliar sensations she was going to experience before the night was through.   Somewhere in the turmult of her mind, she realised that Jace was very skilled in his lovemaking. His deft, knowledgeable hands caressed and explored every niche of her body, stroking away the vestiges of her inhibitions until she was ready to totally surrender to his amorous demands.

Reminding himself that this was Tammy's first experience with lovemaking and that he was not going to rush her, Jace leaned down and swung her up into his arms, carrying her over to the bed where he freshly bathed her senses in every exquisite delight that a man could give a woman. And when he knew that she was ready for him, he plunged into her incredible warmth with the gentle urgency of a man eager to prove his love to a woman.

The slight pain Tammy had experienced was washed away in a pool of ecstasy as the fierce hunger of Jace's thrusts pushed her slowly and slowly to a point where she could go no further.

She was awed by the dizzying rush of pleasure, such that she'd never experienced before in her entire life. And when Jace joined her in this blissful oblivion, she knew truly that this was the man she would love for the rest of her life.

For a moment longer, they clung together, bonding their emotions before Jace finally released her. Tammy watched as he bent his head toward her, his smile deepening as he laced his strong fingers through hers.

'Happy?' he whispered.

'Happy,' Tammy answered in return.

Snuggling against the heat of Jace's chest, she closed her eyes and drifted into a hazy dream about a house and children, and the handsome man whose future she would share forever.

Dear Reader

We hope you have enjoyed this novel. At Peacock Publishing, we are committed to providing you with the very best in romantic fiction because you, dear woman of culture, truly deserve the best.

Therefore, we would ask you to take time out to complete our questionnaire below and return it to the specified address. To show our appreciation, if you are purchasing the AFRODERMA product advertised, we will allow you to qualify for a £3.00 discount on the product. Simply return this questionnaire with your order.

When answering questionnaire, please tick one option per question unless otherwise stated. Thanks for helping us to serve you better.

1.   How did you find this novel?

a   ☐   Excellent - I couldn't put it down.
b   ☐   Good - I wasn't bored with it.
c   ☐   Okay - It could've been better.
d   ☐   Bad - It did nothing for me.

2.   Which age category do you come under?

a   ☐   Under 16
b   ☐   16 - 21
c   ☐   21 - 30
d   ☐   31 - 45
e   ☐   Over 45

3.   What is your career option?

a	☐	Model	j	☐	Actress
b	☐	Air hostess	k	☐	Novelist
c	☐	Journalist	l	☐	Singer
d	☐	Nurse	m	☐	Secretary
e	☐	Teacher	n	☐	Artist
f	☐	Designer	o	☐	Own Boss
g	☐	Director	p	☐	Politician
h	☐	Scientist	q	☐	Astronaut
i	☐	Florist	r	☐	Other

4.   How often do you read a novel?

a   ☐   Daily
b   ☐   Weekly
c   ☐   Monthly
d   ☐   Infrequently

5. How much do you spend on haircare products in any one month?

a ☐ Over £5.00/$10.00
b ☐ Over £10.00/$20.00
c ☐ Over £20.00/$40.00
d ☐ More

6. Would you read another Peacock Novel?

a ☐ Yes
b ☐ No - Why not ....

7. Which skincare product/brand do you mostly use on your face?

....

8. Do you buy any magazines monthly?

a ☐ Yes - Which ones? ....

b ☐ No - Why not? ....

9. How much do you spend on skincare products in any one month?

a ☐ Under £5.00/$10.00
b ☐ Over £5.00/$10.00
c ☐ Over £10.00/20.00
d ☐ Over £20.00/$40.00

10. How many people on average read your books/magazines?

a ☐ 1
b ☐ Over 2
c ☐ Under 5
d ☐ Over

11. How much do you spend on cosmetics in any one month?

a ☐ Under £5.00/$10.00
b ☐ Over £5.00/$10.00
c ☐ Over £10.00/20.00
d ☐ Over £20.00/$40.00
e ☐ More

salon styled black wetlook curls, slanting hazel eyes and the low neckline dress he considered too revealing of her walnut brown body. 'How much is it costing the company to entertain this legless character and the seventy others back in there?'

Tammy's breath caught in her throat. Calvin had obviously administered the right tonic if this was the kind of temperament he himself had witnessed. 'I don't know who you are,' she chided, her voice dangerously controlled. 'But if you don't leave these premises in precisely five seconds, I'll arrange to have you thrown out.'

'Thrown out?' the newcomer repeated indignantly. 'Strong words to sling at the only person who's been at your grandmother's bedside since three o'clock this afternoon.'

Tammy's eyes widened. 'What?'

'Your grandmother was rushed into hospital. The doctors have her under close observation. And by the way,' he added glibly. 'The name's Jace Washington. I daresay you've heard of me.'

Tammy's body stirred in blind panic.

She'd heard of him alright. Who at Caswell Cosmetics hadn't? Calvin had consistently passed the word that Jace Washington was no longer a threat to the company. Caswell Cosmetics will always be controlled by a Caswell he'd bragged. Now seeing Brazil's most renowned entrepreneur, travelling in Calvin's own private elevator as they descended to the car park, made Jace Washington seem as dangerous as ever.

'Your brother must be losing his grip,' Jace spoke with his eyes trained on the flashing numbers of the passing floors. 'It was obvious from his expression tonight that he assumed I was still in Brazil.'

Tammy kept her expression neutral as she forced back the tears that threatened. 'My brother has no interest in your global movements.'

'For a man in his position, that's hardly very prudent

now is it?' Jace mocked, absently smoothing the shadow of a moustache that framed his upper lip.

'And what position is that?' Tammy quipped.

'Your grandmother's latest attack could seriously undermine his position in the company. With my share holdings, I think he should consider . . .'

'Calvin will only consider defeat when it seems imminent,' Tammy interrupted rudely.

'Imminent is just on the horizon,' Jace seemed sure of himself.

'You're very brash and abundantly ill-mannered,' Tammy admonished madly. 'My grandmother has survived two such previous attacks. She happens to be a very strong woman, despite her frailing years, so I'd gladly ask you not to treat the situation as terminal. Not at least . . .'

Tammy pressed her hand against her mouth. Suddenly the thought of anything happening to her grandmother seemed ever more frightening, but Jace's eyes narrowed in on her nonetheless and hardened like iced cocoa.

'I have no wish of treating your grandmother's attack lightly,' he told her in a low threatening tone. 'I have known Hattie Caswell since I was a little boy and respect her immensely. As for her fading health, I blame that on you and that playboy brother of yours. His private and well reported female conquests of late and your frequently publicised client-hunting parties have contributed a great deal.'

The elevator doors swung open and Tammy stepped out into the dimly lit car park, amassing every inner strength she could muster to regain her self-assured composure. 'I'll not let you intimidate me,' she peeved, her voice weak with guilt. 'Your block purchases of Caswell stock, indicative of a hostile takeover, have been equally responsible.'

'When the chips go down,' Jace challenged savagely. 'I think your grandmother would prefer to rest assured with the fact that Caswell Cosmetics were left in good hands, my hands. That I will promise you.'

On their way to the hospital, Tammy thought ruefully how Jace Washington could achieve precisely that. Over the past few months, he had gained large quantities of Caswell stock which had, a month ago, grown to more threatening proportions. He was slowly moving in to take over the company and her grandmother's illness made that option seem ever more possible.

In truth, she knew Calvin couldn't handle the company and she hadn't the experience or the capability to repeat her grandmother's successful business transactions which had begun 30 years ago from a small shop in North-East London.

Now she felt nothing but shame over her continued absence at company board meetings and more accurately, at her own office desk. She knew Jace could use that to his own advantage and with the addition of Calvin's performance, he had good leverage to whip up support for a takeover.

She and Calvin would have to tread very carefully until they knew exactly what card Jace Washington intended to play. With that in mind, they could strategize a move to save the company from his grasp.

THEY ARRIVED at the private intensive care establishment on the top floor of the three-storey hospital building. Tammy tried desperately to force down her rising anxiety as they entered the reception area and confronted the trained uniformed nurse.

For the second time in her 26 years, she succumbed to the frightening fear of enduring yet another loss in her life, second to that of her parents, victims of an automobile accident ten years ago. Now, the dynamic, dominating personality known famously in the world of afro cosmetics simply as Mama Hattie, seemed destined to give her further heartache and Tammy could only pray she would cope, come the worse.

'You must be Miss Caswell,' the nurse who greeted them smiled with relief. 'Your grandmother has been very problematic and demanding.'

Tammy forced a courageous smile. 'Can I see her?'

'Please do,' the nurse suggested. 'She's suffered a mild stroke, her third I believe?' Tammy nodded. 'We'd like you to persuade her to get some rest. The senior registrar will see you afterward.'

'Thank you,' Tammy replied as she made haste toward the private ward the nurse had indicated. She sensed that Jace Washington was in slow pursuit behind her and found, to her chagrin, that she needed his human presence, no matter how discomforting.

Hattie Caswell was sat propped against six pillows as they entered the semi-large four window room. A smile immediately crossed her fragile features as she watched her grandaughter enter.

'Tammy! Me have no idea that you did even know my favourite godson Jace,' Hattie whispered in her soft Caribbean lingo, her tied brown eyes straying toward Jace's towering six-foot frame. 'The nurses no let me have a telephone. Me did want to order some champagne.'

'Champagne!' Tammy wavered a brave smile in curiosity, eclipsing her amazement over the new knowledge that Jace was infact Hattie's godson. 'Grandma, you're not intending to celebrate your stroke?'

'Chu,' Hattie replied with a wry grin as she discreetly removed the hairnet from her thinning grey hair. 'You know me a talk 'bout your engagement to Jace.'

'Excuse me?' Tammy said finally, having found her voice.

'Well me know it's a secret,' Hattie enthused weakly, reaching for her brush by the bed cabinet, 'and me nah a go tell nobody, but you should have tell me.'

Tammy glanced at Jace and found him watching her with such mock sincerity, she had hardly the grace to deny it. 'We didn't want you to get over excited,' she assured quickly, her mind reeling on how Hattie had come across such a plausible lie. 'And right now, we'd like you to do as the nurse asked. Please try and get some sleep?'

'Come see me tomorrow,' Hattie demanded softly, pointing with her brush to affirm her motherly status. 'A wedding needs careful organization and me want to know exactly what you have plan.'

'Of course grandma,' Tammy promised, now deducting that this could only be the work of Jace Washington. 'Now please rest.'

'Me going to try get little sleep now,' Hattie promised.

It was only moments later, after they'd kissed Hattie goodbye and had consulted with the senior registrar who'd advised that her grandmother be kept reassured and happy, did Tammy confront Jace with the venom he deserved.

'You're really not expecting me to agree to this - this marriage?' she boomed numbly, her senses still churning from the shock of it. 'This is, of course, your idea? I gathered as much from your deathly silence. Well, we've only just met and I'm not about to have my life mapped out by you.'

'Don't flatter yourself,' Jace drawled. 'I have no designs on you becoming my wife. I simply made the only positive move that would put your grandmother's mind at ease. You heard what the doctor said and until she makes a full recovery, that's the way it's going to be.'

'I refuse to go through with it,' Tammy retorted.

'Don't behave like a selfish little bitch,' Jace retaliated furiously. 'Hattie has worked herself into exhaustion because she has two grandchildren who are incapable of handling the company affairs. The least you can do is secure the shares on the stock market by agreeing to this engagement until she regains her health.'

'How dare you talk to me like that?' Tammy felt sick with guilt, anger and rage.

'I don't like it as much as you do,' Jace declared, 'but

think of it this way. You'd be preserving the lifestyle both you and your lazy brother have grown accustomed. Tell me,' he added as an afterthought. 'Did that black off-the-shoulder you're wearing annonymously come out of the company's expenses account?'

The slap was clean, swift and sharp. For the second time in her life, Tammy had administered a blow that spoke of her pride and womanhood. Yet, she was filled with the knowledge and self condemnation that somewhere in Jace's arrogant speech, he had hit a cord of truth.

'I'll not apologise for that,' she said in a shaky breath. 'If we have to go through this pretense and assimilation, so be it. My grandmother's health and tranquility matters very much to me, but that's as far as it goes.'

Jace's swift grip on her arm was firm and hard. 'I'll let you get away with that as I did your brother,' his voice was iron cold. 'Hattie's been very good to me and has often contributed to my education. So if her health means we go right to the altar, then *that's* as far as it goes.'

Tammy watched as his dark eyebrows knit and immediately decided not to retort. Instead, she relunctantly followed Jace over to his BMW, seating herself in the passenger seat as her mind strayed to where Calvin could have got to.

Jace took little time in getting her home, walking her to the very door of her Kensington apartment. 'I think you ought to know that our engagement will be announced in *The Carribean Times* tomorrow morning,' he informed her casually. 'I took the precaution of taking care of that before . . .'

'We'd even met,' Tammy interrupted coldly. 'No doubt you've also arranged announcements in the national newspapers so that I'd be left with no choice?'

'I think you'll find it to be a good business decision when the news reflect on the value of your stock holdings.'

'What you mean is that Caswell Cosmetics will be more secure in the hands of Washington International

Limitada?' Tammy jabbed.

'Something like that,' Jace jeered. 'Incidentally, from now on, we'll have to keep up appearances for the sake of the media and the stockholders, so I'll see you tomorrow morning, around ten. We'll go to the hospital first.'

Not if I can help it, Tammy thought as she later slammed the front door behind her. She was immediately confronted by a furious Calvin who, judging by his expression, had obviously expected her back at least an hour ago.

'Where have you been?' he demanded, his face hot and flustered. Tammy had never seen him like this. His black, well groomed dreadlocks were tied back, but unusually ruffled, his grey designer suit hung loosely about his thin lofty frame and his steel-rimmed glasses was perched so precariously on the edge of his nose that she wondered seriously whether he'd been drinking.

'Where have *I* been?' She quipped. 'Where have *you* been? I expected to see you at the hospital.'

'So you've heard,' he retreated, smoothing his beard nervously. 'Damn Jace Washington. I thought he was still in Brazil.' He ran a shaky hand along his dreadlocks. 'I'm sorry I used the spare key to get in here sis. How is grandmother?'

'Calvin, I'm scared,' Tammy confessed, tears now stinging her eyes. 'She didn't look at all herself. You should have been at the hospital.'

'I went to see Jason Lee,' Calvin lit up a cigarette to camouflage his nerves. 'Things are not good sis. Jace Washington has enough shares to demand a seat on the board and if grandmother . . .'

'Dies.' The words hit like a hammer blow on Tammy's sensitive nerves. 'Calvin,' she didn't know how to begin. 'Jace Washington and I are engaged. Grandma looked a lot happier when we told her and . . .'

'Engaged!' Calvin thought for a minute. 'When did this happen? No, don't answer that. Has it been announced in the papers yet?'

'Tomorrow.'

'Good.' He breathed a sigh of relief and immediately took refuge in a chair. 'That should keep the investors at heel. Whose idea was it?'

Tammy raised an inquisitive brow. 'You support this marriage?'

'That's beside the point sis,' Calvin relaxed. 'What matters is the company, our inheritance.'

'Our inheritance,' Tammy stormed. 'That's all you care about isn't it? Talk about self-interest.'

'Now sis, let's not fight,' Calvin reasoned. 'You and I both know that Jace Washington's company controls and manufactures the largest distribution of Afro haircare products. We have to stick together for a common cause, to keep the investors happy by having them believe that we're considering some form of association with his firm.'

'I thought we'd stick together against Jace Washington,' Tammy boomed. 'Not be in favour of his rash decisions.'

'So he came up with this little stunt. Maybe I've misjudged him.'

'You're unbelievable,' Tammy sighed inwardly. 'Your allegiance is untrustworthy to say the least. Well big brother, I plan not to take this stunt, as you call it, to the altar.'

'But sis,' Calvin began calmly. 'Think of all that's at stake. It's only a small sacrifice. Besides, Jace is not a bad looking guy. Just your type I'd have thought.'

'Looks are not everything,' Tammy chided. 'I've heard he's unprincipled, a libertine and personally, I find his manners intolerable.'

'Sounds like you like him,' Calvin joked pretentiously. 'Let me know when the wedding is.'

Tammy picked up the nearest thing she could lay her hands on, a cushion, and slung it at her brother. 'I blame you for this,' she yelled. 'If you want to hold on to your precious corporate chair and maintain that position you pride so well at Caswell, then I suggest you sharpen your wits and find a way of getting me out of this pickle.'

Calvin frowned inwardly and allowed the smile to drop from his face. 'Listen sis,' he sympathised. 'You know I wouldn't want you to do anything you're not comfortable with. You're my kid sis. Truthfully, I don't think you have anything to worry about. Rumour has it that Jace Washington is dating Sherelle Tate.'

'Sherelle Tate?' Tammy repeated. 'That name sounds familiar.'

'It should,' Calvin confirmed. 'Her debut hip hop album just made number one in the US dance charts last month. It may get her a Grammy Award and she's already tipped to co-star with Eddie Murphy in a . . .'

'Save the résumé,' Tammy swallowed her envy. 'If they're an item, then maybe you're right.'

Calvin rose from his chair. 'I have a party to wrap up so I'll see you tomorrow sis. At the office maybe.'

Tammy watched as he put out his cigarette and added as an afterthought. 'I think you'd better make that a certainty,' she advised. 'I want to know exactly where we stand.'

The events of the night were all she could dream about as Tammy later sank her head into her pillow. Tomorrow, she would be publicly announced as Jace Washington's fiancée, a move to keep the legacy of her grandmother with a Caswell and to scotch rumours of any instablity within the company.

She tossed her head. Jace's arrogance had ignited enough flares of contempt within her, yet deep inside, his physical attraction, success and domineering personality ignited another flare of something she couldn't quite fathom. It was enough to put Tammy on guard, for although she was determined never to yield to Jace Washington or his hair-raising plans, she wondered how she could succeed when she was also determined to keep her grandmother sated and happy.

CHAPTER TWO

IT WAS precisely 10.00 am when Tammy heard the sudden shrill of the doorbell from her bedroom. Still dazed with sleep and fighting the dull ache behind her eyes, she relunctantly got out of bed and slipped into her bedcoat. When she answered the door, it was to stare in profound annoyance at the man whose tall frame seemed to fill the entire entrance, dwarfing her five feet eight.

Dressed formally, with a briefcase in one hand and a small velvet box in the other, Jace looked every bit the busines tycoon the tabloid press had constantly described of him. Tammy peeved at the thought that his timing was uneeringly punctual and observed the wry grin on his face as he handed her the small red box.

'What's this?' she asked tautly, one hand taking the box he offered, the other discreetly pulling her peach silk bedcoat over the skimpy co-ordinating nightdress that barely concealed her slim bodice.

'Open it and see,' Jace urged, inviting himself into her apartment and closing the door behind him.

'A ring!' Tammy's voice was weak to her own ears as she opened the box and stared at the huge diamond solitaire.

'We don't want your grandmother to get suspicious, now do we?' Jace mocked, depositing the briefcase to remove the ring from its box and deftly placing it on her relevant finger. 'I took particular care in choosing something that would meet with your grandmother's approval.'

'This doesn't prove that you have any hold over me,'

Tammy said bitterly, relunctantly admiring the ring's accurate fit.

She immediately saw the remorse in Jace's eyes and was contemplating in taking delight at having caused it, when his hands suddenly slid beneath her silk clad arms and gently pulled her to his rigid steely frame.

Within seconds, his mouth covered hers, moving and probing in a kiss that was lazily coaxing, yet breathtakingly insistent. Tammy tried to break free from his grasp, but the moment his tongue delved into her mouth, she lost all thought of resisting. With a smothered moan, she leaned into him and allowed him to part her lips. Jace's response was instantaneous. His tongue plunged into her mouth and moved playfully against her lips as he stroked and tormented her with desire. A volcano of passion erupted inside Tammy; her body arched against him and her hands lifted compulsively to Jace's neck where she instinctively smoothed and caressed the soft hair at his nape.

Nothing existed except the sensual male lips locked fiercely to hers. When Jace finally released her, Tammy leaned her forehead against his shoulder her lungs gasping for breath as every nerve in her body sensed that she'd been branded, labelled and marked as his property.

'We'll see who has control over whom,' Jace whispered huskily, his warm lips drifting across her cheek downward to teasingly nibble at her neck as his hand began to tug at the belt of her nightgown. 'Where's the bedroom?'

Tammy stared in paralysed terror at Jace's heavy-lidded eyes and retreated two steps backward. 'What do you mean?'

Jace looked at her levelly, sensually appraising every inch of her thinly concealed walnut brown body. 'That's a very stupid question.'

Tammy's fury rose to the boil. 'You egotistical, licentious . . .' She stopped long enough to draw a steadying breath. 'This pretense engagement is precisely that. Pretense. It doesn't give you any rights, liabilities, or temporary lease to my affections or my body.'

She marched into the kitchen and put the kettle on preparatory to making coffee. She was acutely conscious that Jace had followed her in and turned to find him standing in the kitchen doorway, watching her.

'What if we were to marry?' he queried icily. 'I meant what I said yesterday and it's only right that I should sample the goods first.'

Infuriated past reason, Tammy decided to strike back at his male ego. 'Then I suggest you call Sherelle Tate,' she jabbed. 'Old goods are by far what you deserve.'

Jace's jaw tightened. 'Who told you about Sherelle?'

'So it is true,' Tammy smiled with elation over Jace's alarmed expression. 'Does she agree with this little off-the-record arrangement that we have? I'm sure she doesn't,' she nodded knowingly.

'That's none of your concern,' Jace evaded. 'Sherelle has no part in this and I'd like it to remain that way.'

'The old double standards,' Tammy concluded. 'Well, think on. The next time you attempt to take liberties with me, then I think Sherelle has every right to know exactly what her lover is doing.'

Jace raised a savage inquisitive brow. 'Is that a threat?'

'Consider you've been forewarned,' Tammy answered. 'I don't like men who try to have both worlds, especially men like you.'

'Spoken like an experienced woman,' Jace mocked intolerantly.

'What's that supposed to mean?' Tammy snapped, disliking the innuendo he implied.

'Your party-hopping lifestyle hasn't skipped my attention,' Jace declared. 'Both you and Calvin have done much to friviously exploit the Caswell name socially. It's little wonder that one can only assume that you're a learned woman in areas where men are concerned.'

'You're crude and grossly out of line,' Tammy stormed in mounting fury. 'I'll have you know that I'm still a . . .'

She cut herself dead. She was about to say a virgin, but judging from Jace's frank attitude toward sex, Tammy thought he would be the last person to ever suspect that.

'Still what?' she heard him demand.

'Still a single woman,' she boomed after thought. 'And whilst I'm forced into this conversation and this engagement, you may know now that I expect to still carry that status. You're not my significant other.'

Jace looked amusingly confused. 'I'm not a . . ? What am I?'

'Not my significant other,' Tammy repeated. 'Not my lover, not my love interest, and definitely not anyone that I care about outside of a marriage. I'd rather be a spinster for the rest of my life than be linked romantically to you.'

Jace's eyes were unreadable as he leaned against the kitchen door, his arms crossed over his chest, his expression contemplating. When he finally spoke, it was as though the earth had shook.

'At the risk of repeating myself,' he hissed, 'we are announced to be married. That means your very domane is pledged to me for the duration and until your grandmother makes a full recovery, your status is most definitely betrothed.' He pulled a folded piece of newspaper from his inner jacket and slapped it onto the kitchen table. 'I'll wait for you in the car,' he said, already striding out of the kitchen.

Tammy heard the front door slam behind him and with trembling fingers, picked up the newspaper article and read it. Their engagement was confirmed more boldly than any scoop she'd seen in recent days, not listed in the classified columns as she'd imagined. The headline read:

'WASHINGTON JR PLUCKS CASWELL ROSE TO SET AMONG FLOWERING EMPIRE'.

The entire page was devoted to commentary about their enagement and impending marriage. In the centre were two pictures, one of Jace and one of herself, which looked suspiciously like a photograph taken from the family album.   She wondered how the newspaper came by it and loathingly put that down to Jace and Hattie.   Only her grandmother had a copy of that post-graduate snap.

She was much younger then, 22 years old.   Her hair was shorter too, not the shoulder length wetlook as it was now, but her prominent hazel eyes and walnut brown complexion, a legacy from her Afro-Caribbean roots, remained intact.   Except for a nose she considered too broad and a childhood dimple still evident on one cheek, Tammy took pride over the fact that she hadn't physically aged a great deal.

She glanced at the professional shot of Jace.   Masculine strength was etched into every feature of his proud cinnamon profile, from his arched thick brows, his flat-top styled semi-relaxed hair to the cleft carved in his square chin.   The caption said *'Afro-Brazilian entrepreneur, Jace P Washington Jr'.*   She wondered what the middle initial stood for.   In that brief moment, it added an exciting enigma to his character which she quickly ignored.

She refused to submit to his good looks or to the knowledge that the kiss he'd given her was enough to send her through an emotional cyclone.   In Jace's mind, she was available and experienced and Tammy could hardly knock him for that assumption.   After all, she had done very little to protect her virtue as a virgin by parading around in provocative fashionwear and co-hosting enough parties to classify her a wanton woman.   And now by kissing him, she'd only succeeded in underlying that theory further.

But that was of no matter now.   Her only thought was how she was going to get out of their engagement without seriously undermining her grandmother's health or causing explosive headlines that could damage the value of the company stock.

She placed the newspaper back on the table and looked at the diamond ring on her finger.   It represented everything she believed in a relationship.   Love, marriage, children . . .

To live a lie would destroy that very belief. Somehow, she had to break off their engagement before the situation got out of hand.

'WHAT KEPT you?' Jace peeved as he ignited the engine when Tammy had entered the car.

Tammy slammed the passenger door shut and smoothed the crease in her white tailored trousers. 'I had to get dressed, remember?'

Jace didn't respond. Instead he surged into the early morning traffic without so much as another word. The journey was spent in total silence until the car pulled into the hospital entrance.

'By the way,' Jace said so casually that Tammy was put instantly on guard. 'I expect the press will be hounding you soon for a story. They'll probably want to know when and where the marriage will be taking place.' He parked the BMW and cut the engine. 'Just tell them soon and that the location is a secret.'

'And what answers do I give them about our honeymoon plans?' Tammy quipped sarcastically. 'Do I tell them where we're going?'

'Jamaica,' Jace answered, exacting the same menacing tone.

'Jamaica!' Tammy rose from the car and pressed her white handbag beneath her arm. 'You seem to have made a decision on everything. What if I happen not to want to go there?'

'You're impossible,' Jace declared màdly, as he made his way toward the double swing entrance doors. 'I sincerely hope that Hattie makes a speedy recovery so that we needn't worry about a wedding, let alone a honeymoon. That's what you want isn't it?' He marched over to the twin elevators before Tammy had time to retaliate.

Hattie was lying on her side with her back to the door, locked into the FT share index on a portable TV set when Jace and Tammy entered her room. Tammy was alarmed to find her so frail, but quickly forced a smile to her face as she entered.

'Hello grandma,' she quavered, kissing the old lady on the left cheek. 'I see you're already calculating the value that our engagement has had on the stockholdings in the marketplace. How are you today?'

'A little tied,' Hattie answered, immediately seizing Tammy's left hand. 'Sit down and let me look at the ring. Me notice it the moment you walk in here.'

Tammy adjusted the black leather belt around her waist and perched herself on the edge of the bed, expertly camouflaging her deceit as Hattie, like a merchant in precious stones, scrutinised the diamond set delicately against the 24 carat gold band.

'Absolutely beautiful,' Hattie smiled. 'Your grandfather did insist that me wear a diamond ring to.'

'We thought you'd approve,' Jace interjected quietly, leaning against the bedpost. 'I know Manasseh would have liked to have seen his grandaughter engaged.'

'And married with children of her own,' Hattie enthused softly. 'Now me have every reason to get better.' Turning on her back, she allowed Jace to help her sit up. 'Tell me, have unu decided on the dress yet? Me like ivory in preference to white.'

'Ivory,' Jace spoke quickly. 'Tammy's hair will go well with ivory.' He glanced at Tammy and raised a brow, willing her to respond.

'Yes,' Tammy nodded, feeling as though a conspiracy had suddenly erupted against her. 'Ivory it is then.'

'And the dressmaker?' Hattie queried.

'My mother knows a wonderful Barbadian seamstress renowned for her tailored excellence in design,' Jace clarified. 'Maybe you'd like to look at some of her work before you decide. She has an elite catalogue of her collection reserved for such occasions.'

'Tammy?' Hattie edged.

'Yes, why not,' Tammy shrugged, showing little interest.

'No harm in shopping around.'

Hattie pointedly picked up on her grandaughter's disinterest with some concern. 'Wha' wrong Tammy?'

Tammy sighed. 'I don't think we should be organising a wedding while you're ill grandma,' she connived. 'I'd rather wait until you were better.' She saw the derision in Jace's face and chose to ignore it. 'Maybe we should postpone any arrangements until . . .'

'Postpone!' Hattie almost choked. 'Not for me dear. Me want to see you marry and soon, while me still here fi seet. Me owe it to your parents and to Manasseh.'

'Well you're going to get better,' Tammy persisted. 'They'll be plenty of time for you to help me then.'

'That's easier said Tammy,' Hattie reasoned. 'But me a old lady and me a get weak with age. Me want to see you marry. So me insist that you go ahead with your plans. Make me happy.'

A trained nurse discreetly entered the room. 'Excuse me,' she interrupted almost in a whisper. 'It's time for Hattie to get some rest. I'm afraid I'm going to have to ask you to leave now.'

'Of course,' Jace said sternly, firmly taking Tammy by the arm and raising her bodily from the bed. 'We hadn't intended to stay long.'

'But grandma . . .' Tammy protested.

'Come again tomorrow,' Hattie smiled weakly. 'We can discuss the flower arrangements and how you want the reception.'

'Come on darling,' Jace mocked to Tammy. 'Hattie has to rest now.'

Tammy nodded defeated and affectionately kissed her grandmother on the cheek before leaving the room. She walked across to the small reception area and was punching the button to summon an elevator when Jace's hand clamped over her wrist.

'Not so fast,' he growled between his teeth. 'Your little scheme back there didn't quite come off did it? Why don't you just give in and accept the consequences.'

'The consequences being you as my husband,' Tammy scoffed contemptuously. 'I don't want any part of you.'

'You liked me well enough this morning,' he reminded her coolly. 'I don't recall you protesting when I kissed you then.'

Tammy felt her cheeks burn like a red hot tint as she thought of the way he'd expertly kissed her. Even now, every fibre in her body longed to experience again the pressure of Jace's mouth locked demandingly to hers.

'You caught my unawares,' she insisted bluntly. 'And, had I seen it coming, I would have been strong enough to physically resist you, believe me.'

'I see,' Jace quirked. 'Maybe you can convince me the next time.'

Tammy opened her mouth and was ready to launch a counter attack when a familiar voice interrupted her midstream and plummeted her into silence.

'It didn't take you long to gleam what your chances are, did it?' Calvin stepped from the elevator car Tammy failed to see arrive and looked Jace right in the eye. 'A tempting prospect is it, becoming king of the company?'

Tammy suddenly developed a stupified hollow feeling inside her stomach as she gradually closed her mouth and stood in anticipation of a battle that seemed about to ensue.

'What are you babbling on about?' Jace answered wretchedly, the hostility lurking plainly in his face.

'I'm wondering whether you came here for the right reasons,' Calvin boomed. 'It's all becoming evident to me now.'

'And what are the wrong reasons?' Jace queried tightly.

'What would you expect them to be?' Calvin quipped. 'My grandmother isn't getting any younger. Caswell Cosmetics is a lucrative, established operation. Hattie's sudden stroke means she's no longer head of the helm. A man only has to do a bit of fawning and pandering to her wishes by marrying her only grandaughter and boosting the share value at one and the same time to ensure . . .'

Jace suppressed his anger well. 'I ought to punch you in the mouth for that,' he interrupted coldly, his fists clinched and his manner dangerously controlled. 'But I have too much respect for your grandmother to subject her to a brawl outside her hospital room while she is in need of a much required rest.'

'Then I'll see you outside,' Calvin challenged. 'I know you want to take a shot at me so go right ahead. Gives me the opportunity to knock you right on your ass. I didn't hit your hard enough the last time.'

'Calvin!' Tammy cautioned, willing herself to smile as a nurse casually, but suspiciously passed them by. 'This is hardly the place . . .'

'You were right sis,' Calvin interrupted brusquely. 'Your perception is by far better than mine. Jason Lee just told me that there's to be an emergency board meeting next Monday, and guess who's the hot tip to replace our darling grandmother?'

Tammy's mouth fell open as she watched Calvin's face turn toward Jace. 'To be forewarned is to be forearmed sis. Come on.' He took Tammy's arm and pulled her toward the flight of stairs. 'We've got to have a family conference of our own.'

'Tammy!' Jace called over from the elevator. 'I've reserved a table at Carib's Nouvelle tonight for dinner.'

'Cancel it,' Calvin yelled back. 'She's not going to be there.'

Jace pointedly ignored him, though Tammy saw the contempt flare once again in his face. 'I'll pick you up at 8.00 this evening,' he said. 'Make sure you're ready.'

CHAPTER THREE

'HAS HE kissed you yet?' Calvin demanded hotly as he lit up a cigarette in his penthouse. He turned toward Tammy who was seated in one of his oak trimmed chairs, hugging her knees and staring with absent eyes at the portrait of Hattie above his Adam style fireplace.

'No,' she lied instantly, not daring to look at him. 'Aren't you going to ask about grandmother?'

'Can't you see he's trying to butter up the old lady?' Calvin chose to counter her with a question of his own. 'Thank God Jason Lee keeps me abreast of things. What are we going to do sis?'

Tammy felt a little sick. 'I thought your treatment of Jace today was gross. It's not like you Calvin.' Did she really say that? An inbred flinch of conscience told her that Jace's conduct was strictly admirable over the way he'd handled Calvin. Had he been hot-tempered to match her brother's own mannerism, a brawl most certainly would have erupted.

Calvin cursed viciously. 'I hope you're not getting soft on the man,' he told her tautly. 'Just how sick is grandmother anyway?'

'Thanks for the concern Calvin,' Tammy answered sarcastically. 'All she ever talks about is the wedding between Jace and me.'

'Don't worry sis, I'll take care of that,' Calvin chortled sharply. 'You just keep that tyrant away from grandmother okay?'

'What are you going to do Calvin?' Tammy asked weakly. For as much as she disliked the pretense and disparagement of an arranged engagement to a man she didn't love, she feared more the adverse effects the break would have on her grandmother.

'I think I'll give Sherelle Tate a call,' Calvin told her with a tone of menace in his voice. 'Let's see how she reacts when she learns what her lover is up to.'

'But surely she must've read the newspapers?' Tammy reminded, a little confused.

'In Japan!' Calvin exclaimed. Seeing Tammy's alarmed expression, he nodded knowingly. 'Yes. Sherelle Tate is over there promoting her new single, but don't worry sis. By the time I've finished, Jace Washington will have a lot of explaining to do.'

Tammy rose to her feet. 'I think I'd better go home,' she said flatly. 'All this conflict has given me a splitting headache.'

'You're not leaving now?' Calvin said almost frightened. 'I thought you'd share a drink with me. Boy, do I need a white rum on ice.'

'I have a lot on my mind,' Tammy said wearily. 'And, I'd lay off the overproof if I were you Calvin,' she added, already making her way to his front door. 'You're going to need every measure of stamina against Jace Washington.'

As the elevator descended to the ground floor, Tammy thought ruefully how the situation was already steering out of hand. Calvin should rightfully and ultimately succeed Hattie as chief executive of the company, after all, he was blood bonded. Family. A Caswell.

Jace, however, was arrogant, prudent and already revered in the afro cosmetology and haircare sector as a walking success model. Calvin couldn't possibly compete with that. Deep down, she knew that if push came to shove, Jace would be the better man for the job.

She stepped out into the bright noon air, bemused and suspicious. Could Calvin's accusation of Jace be true? Was she really being used as a pawn to win over Hattie's affections and more precisely, her vote? Having Hattie believe that his alliance with a Caswell to continue the legacy of the company was just the kind of thing her grandmother would advocate. Maybe Jace was playing on that. The thought disturbed her a great deal, for in truth, Tammy was beginning to take Jace's act of concern for her grandmother's health rather seriously.

She began to wonder what Sherelle Tate would make of it all. Was Jace's unscrupulous methods and irrepressible lifestlye something Sherelle accepted naturally, or was it all paranoia getting the better of her and Calvin?

Tammy walked the distance to her home, her mind in a dreadful quandary over events as her emotions swayed from the erotic feelings Jace had stirred within her to the motives behind her suspicions of him dabbling with people's lives for his own purposes and gain.

Skipping lunch, she decided to search through her extensive wardrobe for a suitable garment appropriate for a quizzing session with Jace. She was going to keep that 8.00 pm dinner engagement, she decided firmly. She needed answers and a resolution to her treacherous thoughts, if only for peace of mind.

TAMMY KEPT a steady hand as she applied burgundy lipstick and brushed some blusher to her high cheekbones. She glanced at her watch; Jace would be there in ten minutes, she thought, stepping back to survey her full length in the mirrored wardrobe door.

The plain tafetta jade dress with complimentary chiffon jacket pleasantly exposed her womanly curves, but offered very little by way of bodice or cleavage exposure. Even her makeup was thinly covered, brown eyeliner to accenuate her hazel eyes, the lipstick and blusher serving only to enhance her delicate profile.

She brushed her wetlook curls and pinned her hair up into a loose chignon, placing precious gold earrings that had once belonged to her mother into her earlobes for added effect.

Tammy tried to feel pleasure in her appearance, but couldn't. Not when she was about to face the man who'd effortlessly walked into her life and taken it over without so much as a consultation with her. When the doorbell peeled loudly at 8.00 pm navy precise, she nervously smoothed her dress then walked the four yards and opened the Regency style door.

Jace was standing in the doorway, looking every inch the impressive business executive in an attractive slate blue suit and silk tie. His semi-relaxed hair was well groomed, his face freshly shaven, his manner alert.

'That layabout brother of yours isn't here is he?' he greeted her icily, cautiously glancing from side to side expectant of trouble.

'No, he isn't,' Tammy snapped, her mind filled with self-loathing at admiring how attractive Jace appeared. 'And,' she added, 'I'd thank you not to refer to Calvin that way.'

Jace didn't falter, though his eyes sliced over her attire in mock approval. 'I happen to think that's quite accurate and descriptive of your brother.'

'That chief executive position rightly belongs to him,' Tammy protested, deciding to cut to the quick. 'Surely you're not going to accept the post if it's offered to you?'

'That's a decision for the board of directors,' Jace clarified. 'You and your brother will have the chance to vote against me if you wish. The meeting's not until next week, but I should imagine that will give Calvin just enough time to financially bribe some of the members.'

'You knew it would come to this didn't you?' Tammy accused hotly. 'That's why you've been buying up blocks of shares to secure a better standing and that's why we're engaged.'

Tammy half expected him to snap back in his defence, but instead, Jace retreated one step backward as though he'd been struck head on. 'I can't believe you could have such thoughts about me,' his voice was like an icicle. 'That you could be so frank and crudely accusatory. No doubt this is your brother's deduction and your grandmother's health has nothing to do with it?'

'You know my grandmother's health means everything to me.'

'Does it?' Jace questioned. 'I'm beginning to wonder at what lengths you'll go to support that good-for-nothing brother of yours. Did it ever occur to you that Hattie also has a choice?'

'My grandmother told you what she wanted?' Tammy asked weakly.

'Let's just say she'd rather be assured that the two things she cares about most in life - her grandchildren and the company - will be in safe hands.'

'Your hands no doubt,' Tammy said flatly. 'How charitable of you to take on such a formidable responsibility. What do you do for an encore? Adopt orphaned children too?'

'God helps the man who takes you for his wife,' she heard Jace say. 'But as I told you before, as long as Hattie is in that hospital, we keep her happy.'

Tammy was already conspiring on the best tactic to turn the situation around when Jace seized her by the arm. Until that minute, she'd forgotten that they were going out to dinner. 'If we don't leave now,' he reminded, 'we're going to miss our reservation.'

THE SMALL restaurant was dimly lit and crowded with the sort of society people who preferred paying out money for small amounts of food on their plates. Tammy scoffed as the waiter stationed near the door greeted them with a polite *'good evening'*, then proceeded to show them to the only unoccupied polished marble table in the entire place.

She hated eating out. On many occasions, her guarded privacy had been stripped by press photographers who always seemed to be lurking behind a palm tree or just happen to be sitting at an adjacent table. Calvin's well reported affairs were testimony to such cunningness, as were those of their closest friends.

The formally dressed waiter dutifully pulled out her chair and as she walked the short distance, she acknowledged Jace inclining his head toward an expensively dressed woman in her forties and the rather younger woman who she immediately recognised from a magazine article in *Essence*.

'Friends of yours?' she queried, taking her seat to avidly digest the two women and the two rather heavyset men beside them who, she suspected, were close to grazing sixty.

'Trixy is . . .'

'I know who she is,' Tammy admitted about the younger woman, trying not to sound awed over Trixy Stephenson's profession as Paris' top Afro-European model. 'How do you know her?'

'I know her father,' Jace took the adjacent chair.

'I see,' Tammy nodded. She studied the beautiful woman whose age wasn't far removed from her own. Trixy seemed so free-spirited and beamed a girl-of-the-world smile as a photographer discreetly crept by and took a snapshot of her.

'The other woman is her agent, Annabel Coley,' Jace added, seizing the leather bound menu. 'And as for the two men, I don't know who they are. Probably designers. Satisfied now?'

Tammy immediately glanced at Jace and observed the irritation set in his handsome face. 'Don't worry,' she quipped. 'This isn't twenty questions. You're not mine to behold.'

Jace shot her a piercing look, but did not comment. Instead he scrutinized the menu, then said a few seconds later. 'I'm very much yours for the duration if you'll have me.' He continued to study the menu, refusing to raise his head to chart her expression. 'I fancy the special. What do you want?'

Tammy's eyes narrowed in on Jace in curious bemusement, her heart skipping to a different beat. What did she want? The food or him? She tried to read into his granite profile, but his expression gave nothing away. 'I'll - I'll have the fish,' she said quietly, deciding that he was referring to her natural appetite and not her physical hunger.

An older waiter appeared at their table and offered to take their order. Jace took care of the preliminaries, ordering two selections of refreshments to accompany their meal. He poured the clear sparkling coconut wine into two fragile glasses then handed her one before leaning back into his chair. Raising his glass to his lips, he silently contemplated her over the rim.

Tammy rolled the stem of her glass between her fingers, trying desperately to ignore the atmosphere of cool formality and pretense. Taking a fortifying swallow from her glass, she glanced nervously around the restaurant, her mind in thought over what topic could mutually interest them.

Finally, the silence was too much. 'This is ridiculous,' she said irritably. 'We've been here for fifteen minutes now and have absolutely nothing to say to each other.'

Jace eyed her speculatively. 'What do you want to talk about?'

'I don't know,' she shrugged helpless. 'Anything. Surely Caswell Cosmetics isn't the only thing . . .' She paused as the waiter arrived and placed their plates down on the table.

When he'd left, Jace pryed, 'Do you know Jason Lee socially?'

The meaning Tammy read into those words and the insolence she saw in Jace's eyes implied he was prodding for something beyond friendship. 'You mean intimately?' she clarified annoyed.

'Whatever.'

Her lips pursed into a hard line. 'Why?'

'He was asking about you today. Told me he'd be calling on you later.'

Tammy picked up her spoon and toyed with the hot peppered goat fish soup. 'I don't intend to question you about your private life,' she told Jace curtly. 'The least you can do is not question me about mine.'

'Am I at least likely to be faced with any jealous opponents?' his lazy voice pressed. 'Your brother is about as much as I can deal with.'

'Calvin is only protecting what is rightly his,' Tammy answered defiantly. 'Caswell Cosmetics is vulnerable right now, not just because of grandma's illness. Our newly launched Ebon makeup range is not doing very well because we suffered a recession last year and . . .'

'You haven't answered my question,' Jace interrupted with an inquiring lift of his brows.

'No. You're not open to confrontation with any infinitely eligible bachelors,' she stated tersely. 'Satisfied now?'

'Just checking,' Jace grinned at the double entendre before biting into his piece of roasted yellow yam.

'You should have done that before you decided to announce our engagement,' Tammy said repressively. 'Is it your general consensus to tempt Providence by getting involved with a woman you hardly know?'

Jace laughed. 'I've read enough about you. Let me see.' He rubbed his cheek playfully to purposefully assimilate pain. 'First there was the clean slap you gave Des Powell, president of the Soul Roots beauty salons. Right across his face, if I heard correctly, at one of your legendary parties. Unlike the one you gave me, that was widely publicized I believe as far afield as the New York *Amsterdam News*.'

'That was a mistake,' Tammy informed him blithely, regretting miserably the occasion on which she'd lost Caswell such potential business. Calvin still hadn't forgiven her and neither had Des Powell. He'd coaxed two other clients to withdraw their contracts until he personally received an apology and though she'd conceded, it failed to reinstate his interest in them as suppliers.

'Then there was Calvin's alleged paternity suit to which he sued one of the national press for libel,' Jace continued aloud. 'You were pictured by his side and, if my memory serves me well, was reported to have, I quote, *'branded Helena Stuart a liar'* unquote.'

Tammy's delicately moulded cheekbones burned with shame as she recalled supporting Calvin against the Afro-American sitcom actress who'd conspired to accuse him of fathering her unborn child. It was later proven that Calvin was not the biological father and that, in turn, earned him damages from the disparaging newspaper.

'I've had the dubious pleasure of reading about you too,' Tammy said coolly, refusing to allow Jace to drown her with her own scandalous past. 'I know all about your torrid affairs and intimately brief relationships. I also know that you specialise in seeking out companies to buy cheaply, then sell off large chunks at a profit to help pay off the debt you've incurred for the purchase. You've shot to prominence by dismantling fine companies that could well have been saved by investing in equipment, research and development.'

'I see,' Jace spoke sternly, the icy blast evident in his gaze. 'So I'm an amoral jet-setter and you're miss goody-two-shoes whose elusive lovers have expertly managed to out-wit the press. Well Miss Caswell, I don't accept biased judgement from a woman who hasn't got a head for business, who's just as promiscuous and especially one who cannot even attempt to utilise her own office.'

His words forced Tammy to lean back into her chair, the guilt rising to burn through her unblemished profile. 'I go to my office every now and then,' she explained lamely. 'The work still gets done.'

'On schedule?'

'Well . . .'

'Precisely what I thought,' Jace interrupted knowingly. 'Just the kind of pressure which has attributed to putting Hattie into a hospital bed.'

'I wish you'd stop appropriating blame for my grandmother's condition,' Tammy forcefully suppressed her conscience. 'If blame be spread, I've watched her age attempting to discover the mystery bidder for Caswell shares. It turned out that you were responsible for our two consecutive raids.'

'And you think my only purpose is to asset-strip the company for profit?' Jace concluded evenly.

'If your history is anything to go by, yes,' Tammy admitted coolly, reaching for her wine glass. 'Acquisitions have fuelled your company's growth. Without them, your profitability brakes to a snail's pace. As for my promiscuity,' she interjected, bridging the glass on her lips. 'I have the same right as you to satisfy my physical desires with whomever I wish.'

She was about to wash down the dry taste of enmity on her tongue when Jace seized her arm. In an instant, he had snatched the glass from her hand and placed it on the table. 'Let's get it over with so that I can stop wondering,' his hand tightened around her arm. 'How many have there been?'

Tammy stared at him. 'How many what?'

'Lovers!' Jace spat back.

Tammy could hardly believe her ears. From the moment Jace had met her, they had been in conflict over her freedom to ascertain her rights as a single woman. Of course, if he were to know that she was a virgin, it would knock the breath and fight out of him. But Tammy didn't want that. His whole attitude simply flared her contempt further, that he should misjudge her standards of morality.

No. She would exact her revenge and keep him guessing. The sheer enigma would probably kill him. 'That's none of your business,' she told him grimly. 'My life isn't assigned to you.'

'Don't speak too soon,' Jace warned, releasing her arm. 'You may just find that you are wholly accountable to me.'

The rest of their meal was spent in comparative silence. Neither spoke to the other except when Tammy had asked for the salt. It was as they'd concluded dessert when Jace suddenly reached for her hand. Before Tammy knew what was happening, Jace had brushed a kiss on the tip of her fingernails. She was so surprised, she overlooked completely the warning squeeze he gave her.

'What are you doing?' she hissed beneath her breath, her senses suddenly alert with unwanted joy at the sweet endearment of his lips seductively stroking like feathers against her fingers.

'There's a photographer heading our way,' Jace whispered bluntly. 'He may stop at our table, so be ready to play your part.'

Tammy tensed incredulously, then forced a falsely radiant smile to her face. 'I don't like this,' she gritted weakly. 'I hate cameras.'

'And so you should with your past record,' Jace smiled back. 'Just look into my eyes like you're in love.'

'I can't,' Tammy spluttered. 'I'm not in love with you.'

Jace's jaw tightened. 'Well, remember to whose benefit this is for,' he reminded. 'I'm sure we can both divert the adverse we have for one another until he leaves.'

'You're enjoying this,' Tammy muttered, observing the rugged chisled angles of Jace's jaw and cheeks and then the cool depth of his brown eyes. 'Has he gone yet?' She didn't dare look.

'No,' Jace answered. 'We'll have to be a little more convincing.'

Tammy stiffened. Flirting with Jace was more likely to graduate dangerously toward suggestive teasing. A man of his experience with women could easily turn the situation around so that she could unknowingly be collaborating her own seduction. What Tammy feared more than ever though was her reaction. For as much as their little interlude excited her, she wasn't sure how she would react if Jace touched her. Yet somewhere in the far recess of her mind, she was yearning to take the risk. 'What do you want me to do?' she queried, desperately willing herself to remain level headed.

'Whisper sweet nothings into my ear,' Jace suggested, pulling her arm so she was forced to lean within inches of him.

'I don't know,' Tammy began nervously. 'I . . .'

'For an experienced woman, your bashfulness amazes me,' Jace said scathingly. 'Surely you can manage an unintimate a gesture.'

Tammy straightened in her chair. 'Of course I can,' she quipped, pinched by his ridicule of her. 'Whisper number one coming up. You great big kangaroo. You'll never get me to the altar my sweet.'

'If I were to marry you honey,' Jace whispered in return, 'you can be sure you'd be getting a real man.'

'Darling, your masculinity doesn't impress me,' Tammy lied in response, 'I'd sooner sleep with a ferocious, man-eating crocodile.'

'I've got more teeth.'

'Pervert.'

'And I'm crazy about you too beautiful.' Jace tilted his head and brushed a faint kiss first against her forehead then he moved downward to plant another kiss on the tip of her nose. Tammy felt as if her heart had slammed into her ribcage and for a fleeting moment, she held her breath, helplessly awaiting the physical impact of his lips to meet hers.

But Jace bypassed her lips and began instead to explore the browny soft skin of her earlobe, his warm mouth nuzzling against the sensitive area. Tammy was paralysed to do anything except close her eyes and mentally accept the mass of quivering sensations that ran like hot water along her veins.

When he nipped her earlobe, a current leaped between

them so electrifying, she stiffened with the delicious unexpected shock of it.

'Oh God,' she heard Jace whisper hoarsely under his breath.

'That - that should've floored him satisfied,' she murmured, oddly relunctant, but sensibly averting her neck in an attempt to break free. 'I - I think that photographer more than earned his salary's worth with that shot.' Tammy risked a sidelong glance across the room then immediately alerted her posture. 'Where is he?'

Jace leaned into his chair. 'He left two minutes ago.'

'What?'

'Like me,' Jace told her, 'he was definitely satisfied with what he got.'

Tammy's cheeks burned as her mind replayed the last five minutes. Their performance, although totally fabricated and entirely innocent on her part, must've seemed pretty steamy to an unsuspecting eye. The thought of the scene visually splashed across the morning papers however, left a collection of nerves in the pit of her stomach. 'I'm ready to go home now,' she said finally, her mouth superdry.

'I'm ready,' Jace answered crudely.

'Ready for what?' Tammy quipped.

IT WAS 11.00 pm when Jace finally accompanied Tammy to the front door of her apartment, his eyes watchful as she placed the bronze key into the lock and pushed open the door. Tammy heard him come up beside her and turned to find that he was precariously within inches of her.

Suddenly alarmed at betraying any visual signs of her inner feelings, she stepped into the dim shadow cast by the door, for Jace's very presence immediately sent a tremor of unfolding stimulations that proceeded from her abdomen to her feet; heady and new feelings which she stoically repressed because she had no means of controlling them.

'There's just one thing,' she heard Jace say, her eyes studying his wide shoulders and rugged jaw that suddenly seemed to possess a raw, primitive maleness. 'I won't be able to see you tomorrow morning. I have a prior engagement, so perhaps you'd like to arrange a taxi to take you to the hospital.'

Disappointment ripped along Tammy's nerves as she looked up into the warm brown eyes that glowed like magic in the dark. This was the opportunity she'd waited for, to see her grandmother alone and systematically sow the seeds of allegiance that would ultimately succeed in the wedding being called off.

Without Jace there to conspire against her wishes, Hattie would quietly listen to what she had to say. A one on one conversation would serve her purposes perfectly. So why wasn't she deliriously happy at the chance? 'When shall I see you?' she queried, deliberately trying to keep the equilibrium in her voice. She failed. Jace sensed her disappointment and smiled knowingly. And what a smile. His face was transformed with such devastating charm, Tammy's heart gave an odd lurch.

'I'll give you a call,' he told her triumphantly. 'I took the liberty of asking your secretary for the number yesterday.'

Blood rushed into Tammy's cheeks. She was angered by her own weakness and by the indelible effect Jace was having on her. He was her enemy and had to remain that way if she were ever to succeed in being rid of him. Tilting her chin, she said. 'You had no right to ask for my number and Delores had no right in giving it to you.'

Jace aimed and unerringly caught her chin between his forefinger and thumb. For a moment, he studied her fragile, almost etheral beauty, then rubbed his thumb gently along her delicately formed jawline. 'I'd give you something to dream about if only you weren't so defiant,' he whispered against her lips. 'Maybe next time.'

'I don't want to be seduced by you,' Tammy lied

profusely in response, alerting her subborn stance to prevent herself from sinking deep into the abyss of the moment.

'I've no intention of seducing you,' Jace said with dry amusement, 'so we're in agreement.' He released her chin and turned toward the stairs. 'Sweet dreams beautiful.'

Tammy closed the door behind her and placed an unsteady hand on her heart. It was beating so fast, she feared a relapse. With shaky legs, she made it across the hall into her bedroom and slumped bodily onto her bed.

How could any man be so outrageously self-confident, so arrogant and so utterly wonderful all at the same time? He was everything a man should be; intelligent, assertive, strong, sexy . . .

The telephone by her bed buzzed into action. An unwilling smile suddenly trembled on her lips. Had Jace decided to call her on his car phone to check her number? It was just the sort of thing he would do. A good dose of uncertainty might throw him off balance, she thought reaching out for the receiver. 'Battersea Dogs Home,' she answered flatly.

'Tammy?'

'Calvin!' Tammy flopped down onto her back and gazed at the decorative ceiling, annoyed. 'Do you know what time it is?'

'Obviously you don't,' Calvin bit back. 'I've been calling for hours. Where in the hell have you been?'

'Out,' Tammy answered. 'I do have a social life outside business you know, albeit limited.'

'People like you never have a social life,' Calvin joked. 'You're far too puritanical sis.'

'What do you want Calvin?' Tammy chimed.

'I think congratulations are in order,' Calvin's voice held a certain degree of satisfaction. 'Plan A is in operation. I've just spoken with Sherelle Tate and guess what? She's going to stop over in England on the mid morning flight tomorrow.'

Tammy sat up. 'What?'

'Yes,' Calvin laughed. 'Like I told you sis. By the time I've finished with Jace Washington, he will most definitely have got his comeuppances.'

CHAPTER FOUR

TAMMY AWOKE the following morning with a splitting headache. She hadn't slept a wink the night before as her mind did nothing but fret over Calvin's tactics in contacting Sherelle Tate. She wondered what Jace's reaction would be and deliberated over her own at meeting the woman for the first time. Calvin would obviously be estatic at succeeding in creating trouble, even if it meant that their grandmother ultimately suffered the brunt of his actions.

She got out of bed with heavy feet and headed toward the en suite shower room. As the sensible young Caswell, it was probably her duty to do something to prevent the inevitable confrontation that lied ahead. Firstly, she would have to go and check on her grandmother before proceeding to the office to catch Calvin, hopefully, she thought wearily, before he had time to put his treacherous plans into operation.

IT WAS ll.30 am when Tammy finally entered the hospital. Dressed in a blue crepe de chine suit, she walked up the short flight of stairs and into the entrance lobby. Pressing the button to summon the elevator, she stood and patiently waited for the car to arrive.

'Miss Caswell.' A familiar voice jerked her attention and Tammy turned to find Doctor Millican walking toward her. He was her grandmother's longtime private physician and close friend, and had also been the doctor who'd delivered her at birth. He probably knew more about the Caswells' health than anyone she could care to name and judging by his expression, he had obviously just had a grilling session with her grandmother.

'How are you doctor?' she asked, turning to greet the stout mild mannered man whose spectacles always seemed to be perched far too close to his eyes

'I'm fine Tammy,' Doctor Millican replied with a knowing smile. 'I hear you're expected to be married shortly. July, so I'm told?'

'Er . . . yes,' Tammy responded evasively, clinching her fingers tightly around her blue handbag. 'We haven't fixed a date yet.'

'Oh, but your grandmother has just told me that the date's been fixed for Monday, July 5th,' the doctor responded with surprise.

The blood drained from Tammy's cheeks. She swallowed her breath to suppress the gasp of shock that threatened and stared at the doctor, willing him to repeat what he'd just said. 'I . . .' Her voice failed her.

'Your grandmother was very certain of the date,' the doctor confirmed.

'I was hoping to keep it quiet for a while,' she said at last, consciously forcing herself to remain composed.

'You Caswells can't keep much from me,' the doctor said lightly. 'I know you all too well.'

'Yes,' Tammy answered, her mind elsewhere. A wedding date had been set for her marriage to Jace. How could grandmother do that to her? It was bad enough having Jace breathing down her neck prompting her every move to please Hattie, but now the old lady was doing it for herself.

'July 5th is only a few weeks away,' Doctor Millican reminded sympathetically. 'With your grandmother the way she is, maybe my wife can offer you a helping hand with the organisations. She's very good . . .'

'No,' Tammy blurted harshly, then realising her tone and observing the doctor's startled expression she softened her voice and repeated, 'No. I'm fine, really. I have everything under control.'

But did she? As she hurried into the elevator car, which mercifully arrived in time for her to seek refuge and hide the murderous intent evident on her face, Tammy wondered whether she'd ever had any control at all. Her heart thumped heavily against her ribcage as the doors slid shut. What were she to do now?

Her whole world suddenly felt like it was coming apart at the seams. Jace's lover was arriving in England at any moment, Calvin was plotting revenge on a scale she'd never known possible, Hattie excited herself over a marriage from her hospital bed and Jace collaborated the entire conspiracy to comfortably succeed in heading the company that rightfully belonged to her brother. She was the only drifter, allowing events to happen around her without any self determination.

When the doors slid open, she steadily walked the four metres toward her grandmother's private room. It was time she firmly told everyone where to get off, starting with her grandmother. There would be no wedding, she thought confidently. Jace could go back to Sherelle, Calvin could unselfishly think about co-ordinating his efforts with Jace for the common good of the company, and grandmother would just have to learn to accept her condition and relax without interfering in her grandchildren's affairs. As for her, she'll live the life she's always lived, free from demanding relationships.

Defiantly, she tipped her head and marched into the corner room, but the moment her eyes drifted toward her grandmother, seated in a chair by her bed, Tammy's firmly implanted resolutions subsided. Hattie's features mirrored that of her former self. She seemed healthier than she'd been the day before, her fingers moving feverishly among the snippets of paper littered all around her bed.

Whatever Hattie was actively engaged in, it caused her to tut and mutter to herself in the usual fashion Tammy so often warmly assosciated as her grandmother's trait of ordinance and command. It was a sight to behold.

'Tammy!' Hattie enthused delightfully. Even her voice carried weight and strength to throw her mild octaves across the room. 'Me so glad you set the wedding date.'

'Me?' Tammy reacted a little bemused.

'Yes dear,' Hattie failed to observe her grandaughter's puzzled expression. 'Jace called me this morning and broke the good news. Me a write out the guest list now. Me hope you no mind?'

'Mind!' Tammy gasped, her eyes seeing nothing but the colour red. Of course she minded. Who in the hell was Jace Washington to think that he could make such radical statements without her prior consent or knowledge? Hadn't she told him exactly her position, that she would only play it so far?

Yet, she was forced to acknowledge that without such a facade, her grandmother wouldn't be looking so well presently. Her oval face glowed in shades of tawny gold, her frail brown eyes sparkled like topaz, and although it was plainly evident that Hattie's left arm appeared weak, she was nonetheless positively blossoming with personality.

Could she risk jeopardising such a remarkable development by announcing that she had no intentions of marrying Jace Washington? Without quite hearing the words, Tammy conceded, 'No. I don't mind at all.'

'Good girl,' Hattie fussed, 'because we have a lot to do. First there's the flowers. The bridesmaids! Goodness, we haven't . . .'

'Grandma, slow down,' she cautioned quickly, placing a bag filled with fruit on top of the bed. 'Let's start at the beginning.'

An hour later, Tammy left Hattie to rest - the nurse had arrived and demanded it. Feeling physically exhausted and drawn, but happier at leaving her grandmother in good spirits, she headed for the exit doors. It was only when she'd reached street level did it slowly dawn on Tammy precisely what she'd done. At the time, it hadn't fully occurred to her mind, but now it did. She'd just confirmed all the arrangements for her own wedding.

Tammy placed weary hands against her cheeks and unsuccessfully tried to rub the life back into them. She had to go and see Calvin, right away. Only he could unravel the web of complications that seemed ever to be coiling around her in intricate designs of woven, conflicting emotions.

TAMMY ARRIVED at the Caswell Plaza building just a little after lunch. She stood at the entrance in judgement of the sparkling glass construction that rose up against the stratosphere before entering through the swivel doors.

Nothing had changed in the two weeks she'd been there last. The marble lobby was just as shiny, the flight of elevators still had the usual swamp of African and Afro-American buyers in their grey suits waiting impatiently to be whisked to their destinations, and the army of tinted windows cast the same rays of daylight that invaded the entire area.

She'd often disassociated herself with her grandmother's empire simply because cosmetology wasn't an aspiration that she'd wanted in life which was precisely why she'd avoided coming to her office. But now, as Tammy glanced around with new, appreciative eyes, she suddenly realised that everything Mama Hattie had built meant something to the women of culture who used Caswell products.

It suddenly occurred to her that she and her brother would one day carry that legacy into a new generation. As Calvin had so rightfully pointed out, their inheritance was at stake and it was time she took measures at all cost to protect it.

With that thought firmly implanted in her mind, Tammy walked gracefully toward the elevators and managed to squeeze into the only available car which had just enough room to accommodate her. As the car ascended, she turned sideways to give herself more space and it was at that moment when her heart stopped. Jace was standing right next to her.

Tammy froze with shock, then quickly jerked her body back to the position she'd been previously. Her immediate thought was to turn round and give Jace a piece of her mind over the blatantly false information he'd provided her grandmother with that morning, but to her chagrin, her impulse was to reach up and pat her free hair into place.

Willfully, she quelled her feminine instincts and kept her eyes fixed to the ground. They'd passed the eighth floor. Six people had left the car, but Tammy sensed that Jace was still there, beside her. She wondered if she had a trace of lipstick left or if her face looked alright, then caught herself up short.

For a sensible young woman, she was behaving rather foolishly. After all, she didn't want to impress him with her womanly flair and charm. He was forced upon her and for a relatively short period at that if she had anything to do with it.

The ninth floor went by. Tammy began to find the long ride stifling, although they'd only been in the car for less than two minutes. She wondered if Jace was watching her and found herself cautiously allowing her gaze to slide upward and then sideways to Jace's position. His head was tipped slightly back, his eyes trained on the flashing numbers above him. He seemed different, then she noticed that his semi-relaxed hair was freshly retouched, trimmed and cropped around his face. It fell in nicely with his dark arched brows, his shapely moustache and the arrogant squareness of his chin and jaw. It made him seem more youthful too and his mouth appeared more firm, more sensually moulded . . .

Suddenly his lips quirked as if amusement was lurking there. To Tammy's horror, she suddenly realised that Jace knew she was drooling over him. She risked averting her gaze and almost died on the spot when his warm brown eyes shifted immediately to her. Her fears confirmed, Tammy quickly declined her head.

Simultaneously, the elevator doors slid open and she stepped from the car, hurrying her feet along to be rid of the feeling that her hands had been caught in the cookie jar. Tammy didn't dare look back, but decided to head straight for her office, straight to a place of sanctuary. The footsteps she heard behind her though were indicative that she would not find refuge there.

Halfway down the brightly lit corridor, she heard them stop and then Jace's husky male voice called over to her, 'This *is* your office isn't it?'

A becoming flush swept over Tammy's cheeks so lightly and smoothly, she might have been lounging in a sauna. Her mind had been so trained in thought over how she'd react when Jace finally called out to her, that she had completely overlooked her own office, walking right by the door that bore her name boldly etched in a silver plate.

'I was on my way to see Delores,' she prevaricated, pivoting on her heel to make the two feet back.

'I see,' Jace remarked, silently applauding her wit. 'For a moment, I thought you'd forgotten exactly where your office was located.'

Ignoring his obvious teasing tone, Tammy entered her office, making her way directly toward her desk. Jace followed her in. 'Do you want something?' she flinched, placing her blue bag by the telephone and looking to see where he'd situated himself.

Jace was leaned against the door frame, his arms folded with an evident amused smirk across his clean shaven profile. Tammy wondered warily whether he intended on keeping others out or her in. 'I'd like my curiosity satisfied,' he said drily.

'About what?'

'About why you're here.'

'I've come to work,' Tammy lied. In truth, she'd come to see Calvin to strategize a move against him.

'Really,' Jace chortled in disbelief. 'On a Friday?'

'Any objections?' Tammy chided.

'No. No,' Jace teased. 'Only, I've come to discover that you're the home-grown type.'

'Sewing on buttons for some man I suppose,' Tammy jabbed.

'Buttons come off,' Jace reasoned. 'Someone's got to sew them on.'

'Not me,' Tammy began, purposefully busying herself with the files piled high atop her desk. 'I'd sooner be the corporate type.'

'Oiling your way around a rusty office,' Jace mocked. 'It's certainly accummulated a lot of dust in your absence.'

'My absence will only be at the altar,' Tammy quipped in retaliation. 'Don't think your latest little stunt hasn't gone amiss. You've gone too far setting a wedding date.'

'I haven't gone far enough,' Jace teased suggestively, 'but I intend to.'

'You've also got a one track mind,' Tammy scoffed, observing the sudden intimate smile in his eyes. She profoundly disliked it, for already his lazy gaze was causing a delightful budding sensation to creep upward from her groin to the pit of her stomach.

'You're just annoyed because I spoiled your golden opportunity to persuade Hattie to call off the wedding,' Jace laughed. 'Sorry I couldn't be there to see your face, but I had a salon appointment.'

'I wasn't . . .' Tammy began, freshly detecting that his flat top trim also had a more cropped approach at his sides which framed his face nicely.

'Save it,' Jace interrupted lightly, casually walking toward her until he was within a foot of her. 'I know you better than you think and right now, you want to be kissed.'

'I wouldn't kiss you if you were the last man alive,' Tammy retorted, trying to quell the flutter of mingled apprehension and exhilaration. 'Now if you've exhausted your rappatoir of amusing little quips, then maybe I can finally get down to some work.'

'Tell me,' Jace enquired with a teasing smile on his lips. 'Are you always so aggressive when it comes to men or am I the exception?'

'I don't like men like you who indulge in flippant sexual affairs,' Tammy stated tersely.

'But you advocate women like yourself who do?' Jace challenged obstinately.

'I'm not going to dignify that with a response,' Tammy said a little perplexed. She tried to remain unconcerned and urbane, as if his words hadn't meant anything to her, but they did.

Tammy didn't want Jace to think of her as a corrupt licentious woman. She wanted his respect for her purity and feminine virtue. To attain that though, she would have to tell him the truth and that would mean he'd won. No, she couldn't give in now. Yet, as she forced herself to look at him, Tammy felt her composure slip a notch. 'I'd like you to leave now.'

Jace studied her with narrow brown eyes, absorbing every innocent, almost naive line in her expression. He also digested her raw, tempestuous beauty and the simplicity of Tammy's youthful features, appreciating the quiet poise and proud profile that lent grace to the defiance in her face. He felt puzzled and achingly alive both at one and the same time.

'I'll tame you yet Tammy Caswell,' he said quietly, raking her body in blatant sensuality. 'You'll soon submit to my demands. After all, we're engaged to be married remember?'

'That may be painfully true,' Tammy protested with deceptive scorn, observing the obvious hazy combination of bemusement and deliberate admiration in his eyes that tripled her pulserate. 'But I'm your relunctant significant other, so don't expect me to be civil.'

Jace's fiery brown eyes widened with amusement as he listened to the continued scorn from the alluring female beauty standing before him and in one swift movement, he lunged forward, seized her wrist and jerked her into his arms. 'Civility is the last thing I expect from you,' he whispered before his mouth swooped down and captured her lips in a kiss of savage, hungry insistence.

The instant his mouth touched hers, every fibre in Tammy's body quickened with incredible speed. She was trembling with inner turmoil and the need to feel again the raw, devastating power of Jace's kiss. Yet with a supreme physical effort, she clamped her teeth together and resisted his shattering persuasion, twisting her face away to bury it against Jace's chest. 'Don't,' she heard herself murmur.

Jace's grip eased slightly on her shoulders and when he spoke, his voice was rich with confusion. 'I can't.' His fingers threaded through her hair, cupping her face between his hands so that she was forced to look at him. 'There's something intriguing that makes me wonder about you Tammy. I don't know what it is, but it draws me to you like a magnet and I can't stop it.'

Tammy felt her resistance crumble. Jace's words melted her heart and seduced her to the point of submission. The capitulation was evident in her eyes and her consent trembled in the softness of her lips. Jace paused to behold the angel in his arms before slowly dipping his head to take again what was so freely offered. His tentative mouth covered hers with tormenting persistence, probing to taste the sweetness of surrender that lingered on her lips.

Without knowing it, Tammy's arms closed around Jace's waist and her body leaned against his tall, rigid frame. She felt his strong hands sink into the thick mass of hair at her nape, gently forcing her head back to comfortably cradle into them. His tongue plunged inward, retreated and hungrily plunged again until she instinctively gave him what he wanted.

Feverishly, Tammy began to move her lips with his in a kiss that stimulated a flame that blazed so anew, she was startled by the sheer heat of it. Shudders of pleasure raced along her body in a wild fury and doubled when Jace moaned and pulled her closer still, so close, the pressure of his lips forced her head back to a point that she was forced to break free for air.

Jace beamed a satisfying, triumphant smile as he ran a shaky finger along the contours of her cheekbone, revelling in the thought that he had at last won her over. 'I knew you weren't strong enough to physically resist me,' he said hoarsely, already delving to undo the gold squared buttons on her blue blouse until her lace bra was revealed to his exuberant gaze. 'Have you got a key to that door?'

Tammy drew back instantly, sanity returning quickly to her aid. Her mind suddenly recalled the statement she'd bragged about to Jace the day before and which he now so aptly repeated for her benefit. She also recalled telling him concisely that he had no rights to her body or temporary lease to play with her affections. Yet here she was, a victim of the very thing she'd professed never to indulge in, not at least where Jace Washington was concerned. For, as she suspected, he was taking immense delight at teasing her over the whole matter and she'd be damned if she were ever to allow him to win one over on her. Not after she'd disadvantaged herself and certainly not when he was obviously expecting more from her.

With a sweetly provocative smile that was meant to throughly intimidate him, Tammy said brightly, 'I wondered how far I'd let you go before you got the message that I'm not interested.' She backed away a step. 'I think this is far enough.'

Jace studied her carefully, his expression unreadable as he watched her fingers deftly refasten the very buttons he'd undone a minute earlier. 'What are you talking about?'

'I'm talking about our conversation yesterday morning,' Tammy raised a brow in pretended amazement, indicative that she was startled he hadn't taken her seriously. 'Maybe now you're convinced.'

'This was your idea of teaching me a lesson?' Jace enquired, his gaze freezing over into profound shock.

Tammy kept her smile fixed. 'Yep.'

Jace's jaw tightened. 'For a woman, you play dangerously cold-hearted games,' he said scathingly, the icy chill evident in his voice. 'I have to hand it to you. You had me completely fooled. I sincerely hope your other - playmates can handle you better than I because you certainly need to be taught a lesson in morality.'

Tammy saw the insolence and the hurt in Jace's cold brown eyes and immediately had the overwhelming urge to take back everything she'd said. She hadn't meant to come across so cruelly hard and cynical. Infact she hadn't realised the impact of her impulsive scheme until it was too late to mend the damage. Jace probably hated her now and obviously thought less of her presently than she cared to admit.

'I - I didn't mean to . . .' she began before dissolving into silence. How was she to make amends?

'Didn't mean to what?' Jace hissed icily. 'Initiate me sexually. Spare me the apology, I can take it. I'll be blessedly overcome with relief though when Hattie is finally discharged from that hospital bed so that we need never continue this charade.'

'Which may be any day now,' Tammy snapped back, unable to endure the pain of his words. 'And believe me, the feeling is mutual.'

'Good,' Jace said sharply, making swift strides toward the door. 'In the meantime, there's a charity gala tonight for the Sickle Cell Research Association. Your grandmother normally makes the honours. As a Caswell is expected to be there, I have no choice in the matter but to accompany you. You needn't worry,' he called out, his hand now bridged on the door handle. 'I won't so much as lay a finger on you. I've got the message loud and clear.'

'You can lay a finger on Sherelle Tate instead,' Tammy yelled back, detecting his momentary pause at the door. 'No doubt she'll be there as she flies back from Japan today.'

Jace turned and eyed her, comprehension of her extensive knowledge about Sherelle, angry loathing that she should tell him something he didn't know and enmity over her treatment of him all exposed in his hardened face. Without another word, he turned and stormed out of the room, slamming the door behind him.

Tammy felt a sharp stab of anguish as she went over to her swivel chair and collapsed into the soft leather. She could hardly believe that she'd behaved so appalling, that her resentment could spill over in such magnitude it had even shook up Jace Washington, the man whom a mere whisper of his name was enough to put fear into any boardroom.

Her limbs were still shaking in response to their argument which had portrayed a side to her that she'd never been conscious of before. Could it be because she was feeling more for Jace Washington than simply hate? No, she thought stubbornly. She hated him alright. If she didn't, she wouldn't have behaved the way she had.

Willing herself not to rethink the case of her feelings any further, or what Jace's kiss had done to her sense of wellbeing, Tammy reached for the phone. She'll call Calvin and still execute her plan to oust Jace.

Dialling the relevant extension number, she held patiently on the line then alerted herself when Calvin's secretary answered the call. 'Hello Martha, it's Tammy. Can I speak to Calvin.'

'I'm afraid your brother isn't here,' Martha replied in her usual astute cultured secretarial manner. 'He's gone to Heathrow airport. I think he said something about meeting a very important person.'

Tammy hung up the phone and buried her face into her hands. 'Help,' she murmured quietly to herself. 'Help.'

'Tammy, are you alright?'

Tammy's head shot up and zoomed straight in on Jason Lee who was standing boldly from across her desk. She hadn't heard him enter nor did she sense his presence. He hovered indecisively from across her, fawn eyes looking on in concern. 'I was passing and heard your voice. I didn't know you were coming in today.'

'Impulse,' Tammy nodded, smiling evasively.

'I called on you last night,' Jason said a little embarrassed. 'You were out.'

'Yes,' Tammy nodded again, suddenly feeling awkward. 'I . . .'

'It's obvious from the morning newspapers where you were,' Jason interrupted, his tone oddly possessive as though she owed him some form of an explanation. 'For goodness sake Tammy, why did you have to go and get engaged to the man?'

Tammy rose from her chair and inched toward the beverage table. 'It's a long story,' she mumbled beneath her breath, flinching at the thought of explaining events to Jason.

He had been specially brought in from America to expand their U.S. market operations and had worked with Caswell Cosmetics for over ten years, his loyalty to her grandmother and the firm abundantly excessive. Jason also saw her as perfect prey to fill the void in his life, as he'd never married and had placed the company first for a number of years, much to Tammy's annoyance. Her compassion for Jason had yielded enough to regard him as a friend and she'd gone into his office many a time for iced tea or a quick chitchat whenever she'd graced the company with her presence.

She was dismayed however, when Jason decided to misinterpret her friendship for something more serious, though she could hardly blame him seeing as she'd kissed him once at one of Calvin's pre-Christmas parties. She'd been a little tipsy-turvy for the wine and had regretted the incident ever since. For Jason, anxious for her attention and endeavouring to become a fixture in her family life, as well as her business affairs, cunningly built up an ironcast business relationship with her brother for his support and even became her grandmother's dedicated right hand man.

'Are you going to marry him?' she heard him query from the beverage table.

Tammy turned and saw the panic in his eyes, his five foot eight frame stooping in her direction, braced for her answer. 'The occasion won't arise,' she told him warily. 'It's all completely a fabrication for the newspapers.' She almost heard Jason's sigh of relief and felt a rising anxiety of anticipation.

Jason Lee was attractive in his own right, but he didn't appeal to her. His dress sense was impeccable, his relaxed hair, cut close to his caramel scalp reflected his trendy exterior and the shadow of a beard that became his designer trademark was quite fetching. But he wasn't for her. She didn't want to be unpleasant to him, but she didn't want to become an obsessive part of his life either.

'Are you going to the charity function tonight?' he smiled with renewed hope. 'I can pick you up around 8.30 at your apartment.'

'Jace is taking me,' Tammy confirmed.

He shrugged. 'I thought . . .'

Tammy sighed. 'Jason, you don't understand. 'I . . .' She decided to lie. 'I want to marry Jace. It started out as pretense at first, but now, now I think I'm falling in love with him.'

Jason's eyes shifted uneasily. Tammy knew that through the years he had carved a niche for himself at Caswell and had one day hoped to marry the boss' grandaughter. Jace Washington threatened to change all that and she could see that in his face too.

'I guess I'd better congratulate him,' Jason backed

down, making light of the whole thing. 'And you of course,' he added.

'I'm glad you're taking it so calmly,' Tammy smiled. 'I'd really appreciate your support.'

Jason struggled to remain composed, but something ugly gleamed in his eyes. 'What are friends for,' he smiled faintly.

As he left the room, Tammy tried to decipher his trait. It set a wheel of suspicion to turn in her head, for when Jason and her brother got together, trouble was likely to flare. She wondered further whether she should have made up that story about loving Jace and then panicked over what Jason Lee would make of it. She tried to pretend that she didn't care, he could tell the whole world if he liked. It wasn't true anyway. But even as she tried to deny it, a nagging voice in her head told her differently.

Clasping her handbag from the desk, Tammy made for the door. She couldn't work when so much was going on in her head. She'd go home instead and mull over her problematic life in a jasmine bath. After all, she had a more difficult time ahead of her that night.

CHAPTER FIVE

TAMMY FIRMLY implanted another hairgrip. She momentarily paused to mentally rehearse the way she was going to treat Jace that night, then walked over to her wardrobe and removed a red velvet sheath gown.

She would treat him with the aloof impersonal formality she would the dustbin man or a hospital porter she decided, slipping into the tightly fit dress. That way, she could deflect her real emotions and get through the night without any major personality clashes.

Stepping into dainty silver sandals, Tammy zipped up the dress and went over to her jewellery box. In retrospect, she hadn't expected Jace to behave so hurt and angry over the way she'd treated him earlier. After all, wasn't he the type who involved himself in intimate little escapades with his female prey of the week? Hardly the behaviour of a casanova in a sharp suit. Even now, the upset and the hateful fury that had blazed in his eyes was still unbelievable to her.

Seeking out a pearl choker and matching pearl earrings, Tammy applied the jewellery and went in search of her silver sequinned handbag. Maybe she should attempt at another apology, she thought wryly, fishing the bag from the interior of her wardrobe and dusting it clean. Then, she presumed, maybe Jace wouldn't be so hard on her.

She'd just time to smooth her dress when the doorbell peeled loudly. A fresh surge of anxiety raged through her as Tammy seized her red velvet cape that was lined in silver satin, and made her way toward the door to face Jace. But it was Calvin who was standing in the doorway, looking every inch the corporate playboy in his black tuxedo and tie, specially tinted designer spectacles and his freshly trimmed dreadlocks pulled back more tightly than usual.

'Calvin, what are you doing here?' Tammy asked quietly, exerting a sudden breath of relief.

When he didn't immediately answer, she queried alarmed, 'Is there anything wrong? Grandma hasn't . . .'

His gaze moved over her perfect features and lustrous mass of shining black hair that was caught up in intricate sophisticated twists at the back of her head. With a brotherly look of appreciation, he said, 'Sis, wherever did you get that figure?'

A little bashful and surprised at Calvin's blatant candour, Tammy smiled, 'Calvin!'

'No, really sis,' Calvin insisted, stepping into the hallway. 'I can hardly believe it's you.'

'I thought I'd better make an extra effort,' Tammy said acutely embarrassed. 'Representing grandma tonight isn't going to be easy. I hope you're going to give a good speech when you hand over the company cheque.'

'Well actually sis,' Calvin began, shamefaced. 'I haven't prepared anything to say. I thought maybe you . . .'

'Oh no,' Tammy protested. 'You're older than me. It's *your* responsibility.'

'Couldn't you . . .'

'No!' Tammy admonished firmly.

'Well, come on,' Calvin sighed, making toward the door. 'I've got the car waiting.'

'I can't,' Tammy held back. 'Jace insisted that I go with him.'

'Jace!' Calvin's tone changed at the mention of the other man's name. 'You're still giving him the time of day?'

'What choice do I have?' Tammy bit back. 'I'm getting sick of this play acting myself.'

'From what I hear, you're giving an excellent

performance,' Calvin jabbed.

'That was the general idea,' Tammy retorted.

'Point taken,' Calvin conceded, his eyes suddenly resting on her left hand. 'I see he's given you a sizable rocker. Should fetch a king's ransom when the deal's over. Just make sure you get a pay off too.'

Tammy's eyes widened. 'I'm not keeping the ring if that's what you're thinking,' she told her brother coldly. 'Sometimes Calvin, I find it hard to believe we're related. I have everything I need.'

'Except the love of a good man,' Calvin interjected. 'Time you got married sis and had kids. Make me an uncle.'

'Not with Jace Washington I won't,' Tammy chided, forcing down the cutting edge of truth that sent a shiver of unsettled euphoria to invade her system. 'He's a business shark who enjoys eating up fine companies for breakfast. I shudder to think what he does for lunch.'

'Donate funds for the development of Black education,' Calvin answered relunctantly.

'What?' Tammy looked on bemused. 'Mr Jace P Washington, the amoral jet-setter?'

'Your amoral jet-setter donated eighty thousand dollars to the U.S. United Negro College Fund last year,' Calvin began dispassionately. 'And he's a regular participate and sponsor of the Institute of Research and Black Culture in Rio.'

'I see,' Tammy acknowledged, her conscience reminding her on how she'd hotly accused him of caring only of his company's growth.

'He's from a poor background,' Calvin said without a note of sympathy. 'One can probably admire him for what he's achieved, but I'll not have him head the company that rightly belongs to me.'

'Okay Calvin,' Tammy said quickly. 'I haven't the time for this. Is there anything else you want, only I'd like to freshen up before Jace arrives?'

'Sherelle Tate's in the car,' Calvin confirmed with a forlorn shrug of his shoulders. 'I'm taking her along to the gala. I thought you'd like to know.'

As he left, Tammy tried to decipher the taut set of Calvin's jaw at the mention of Sherelle Tate. Even his eyes seemed to cloud over, almost hazy and intrigued. She wondered what it meant, wondered further why he chose to remind her about her lonesome life, but she didn't have time to ponder. She'd just escaped to the bathroom to freshen up when the doorbell peeled again. This time, Tammy knew definitely who it was.

Jace looked breathtakingly elegant in his raven black tuxedo, snowy ruffled shirt and formal black bow tie when Tammy answered her door. His brown, firm set eyes moved with seductive admiration over her vivid features and travelled slowly downward to the provocative display of her cleavage swelling above the low neckline of her red dress, to the straight skirt which was slashed at the side from below her thigh to the bridge at her heel.

'Are you ready?' he asked with a degree of detached friendliness, the same sort of friendliness he would show the postman.

Tammy handed him her red velvet cape and nodded, suppressing the panic that shot throughout her entire body. It was plainly obvious that he too had decided to treat her with the same impersonal conduct that she herself had decided earlier to treat him.

Judging by his frank, iced cold attitude, Tammy wondered nervously whether she'd see the night through without losing her patience.

THE HOTEL was receiving a good degree of publicity owing to the charitable cause of the function when the BMW pulled up outside. A red carpet had been laid for the special guests and press photographers were positioned at the kerb, each trying to jostle their way to the front, their cameras poised ready to shoot a celebrity.

The instant the doorman stepped forward and opened Tammy's door, his free hand simultaneously hailing a hotel vehicle attendant to come and park the car, flashbulbs exploded on both sides of the kerb and a satellite camera tracked their progress into the building.

Tammy deposited her cape at the coats' desk before she cautiously glanced around the vastly large room, her eyes digesting the animated crowd of at least 200 prominent guests sipping champagne and picking at tropical Caribbean food from a buffet area off-shot the hugh bar.

A waiter politely passed by and openly offered them some champagne. Tammy immediately seized a glass, taking the opportunity to numb the rope of tension that coiled around her chest. Jace was stood within four inches of her, but he made no attempt to move closer as he too accepted a glass.

On the ride to the hotel, he hadn't uttered so much as two words to her, nor did he comment on her appearance or whether he intended on keeping up the pretense of their engagement once they arrived at the hotel. Even now, as they glanced around the room, nodding courteously at familiar faces, his grim expression began to set like quick cement.

The next person she saw caused Tammy's blood to run cold. Calvin was walking directly toward them, a look of ill-concealed glee spread wildly across his face. The beautiful singer who walked alongside him, her hand linked casually over Calvin's elbow, smiled sweetly at Jace as they advanced the short distance between them.

Tammy's eyes shot to Jace, desperately charting his expression. He didn't seem at all nervous, evasive or even acutely surprised. On the contrary, his whole manner remained remarkably composed and questionably formal. Yet when Sherelle put her hand out to greet him, Tammy noticed that he hesitated before acknowledging the greeting.

'You're back early from Japan,' he remarked, slicing his

gaze across the woman's slim bodice, which was clad extravagantly in a soft cream off-the-shoulder attire that complimented her glowing mocha complexion. 'I wonder why?'

Sherelle answered with a chuckle. 'Come on Jace,' she beamed, coaxing for his light-hearted attention as she tossed back her long mane of nutmeg hair with the flick of her fingers. 'I thought that was obvious.' She diverted her attention to Tammy and eyed the younger woman with total indifference. 'Is this the lucky lady I hear you're engaged to?'

'This is she,' Jace answered obligingly.

There was a stupified moment of silence, enhanced by the coveted knowledge that the engagement wasn't at all what it appeared to be. Calvin stood silently at Sherelle's side, his expression itching to involve himself in the conversation, but his mind deciding to remain quiet in the hope of witnessing something spectacular. Tammy nervously studied her manicure, her head downcast as not to see the display of possessive bemusement on the older woman's face.

When Sherelle finally spoke, it was in search of some clarification on the very topic of their engagement which she'd obviously heard about from Calvin. 'Can I speak with you privately Jace?' she queried so quietly, it was almost a whisper.

To Tammy's total surprise, Jace was not about to give the other woman his exclusive attention, whether she deserved an explanation or not. 'Whatever you have to say,' he told Sherelle with a measure of reservation too obvious for comfort, 'you can say it in front of Tammy.'

Sherelle appeared a little horrified, her profile evidently restraining the urge to blurt something right out there and then, but she kept her control remarkably intact. 'It'll keep,' she answered steadily, her pride coming to her rescue. 'Come on Calvin,' her mouth widened into a falsely radiant smile. 'Let's dance.'

As she led the way gracefully to join the animated crowd, practically dragging a disappointed and abundantly shocked Calvin with her, Tammy turned to face Jace. 'How could you treat her like that?' she queried, suppressing her voice as not to attract attention. 'If I were her...'

'If you were her,' Jace interrupted, 'you wouldn't be adding an air of decorum to this room right now.' His brown eyes zoomed in on her. 'Sherelle has no sense of propriety. She would've eaten you alive and the publicity would have been scandalous. I couldn't risk that.'

Tammy opened her mouth, about to tell Jace that she could hold her own with any woman, when the patrons of the charity approached them.

'Jace!' the Ambassadress laughed delightedly, flinging herself into Jace's arms in utter disregard of his drink. She kissed him affectionately on the cheek then withdrew with a hugh smile on her face. 'Why didn't you tell me you were getting married?' she scolded, reaching out to catch her husband's arm and drawing him into the circle of comradery. 'Your mother said nothing to me when I saw her last.'

Jace shrugged and observed the Ambassador's benevolent gaze on Tammy. 'We were very sorry to hear of your grandmother's latest stroke,' the Ambassador said compassionately. 'If there's anything we can do?'

'Thank you,' Tammy answered smoothly. 'She's certainly feeling much better now.'

'I really hope so,' the Ambassadress interjected warmly. 'Me and Mama Hattie go back a long way. Do give her our regards.' Then turning to Jace she demanded, 'Are we invited to the wedding?'

Jace turned immediately to Tammy, his compelling brown eyes searching her face for an answer. In that instant, Tammy wasn't certain of her own name, let alone confirming verbal invitations. Jace's gaze held a certain magical flare, it caused her pulse to race doubletime.

'Grandma's writing out the guest list,' she swallowed, curbing the hoarseness in her voice. 'I'm sure you're on it.'

'Be sure that we are,' the Ambassadress smiled.

'Have you met the host of the charity tonight?' The Ambassador asked courteously. 'I'm sure you know of the American jazz musician, Spike Marsden and his wife. They're both active campaigners for sickle cell anaemia.'

Over the next forty minutes, Tammy braced herself for the inevitable round of introductions that followed one after the other, everyone offering their heartfelt congratulations on her impending marriage. Jace remained civil the entire time, observing her highly effective facade at pretense with a mixture of frank irony and veiled coldness.

From beneath her long charcoal eyelashes, Tammy stole a look at him and shivered at his inner reserve. To her chagrin, she longed to touch him, to run her fingers down his cheeks and trace the cleft of his chin and the shape of his mouth. She longed to feel his closeness too, if only an arm around her waist to steer her among the guests. But Jace kept his drink in one hand, the other in his tailored trouser pocket and remained composed by her side, a strange glitter in his eyes as he watched her immaculate performance with interest.

Tammy realised that she didn't really know much about him; his everyday likes and dislikes, his taste in books or music, or his background growing up in Brazil. Only his dry humour and cold reserve was apparent to her. Yet, although it wasn't easy to clarify her thoughts, she felt very much like she belonged to him. She jerked her gaze away and began to speak to an old friend she hadn't seen in two years.

During the next three hours, they circulated among the crowd, Tammy becoming increasingly nervous over Jace's chilling attitude toward her. He made an unemotional offer to dance and she accompanied him to the floor, but even then, as they moved in time to the Reggae

Philharmonic Orchestra, Tammy vibrantly aware of his legs shifting intimately against hers, Jace's only few words to her were, 'You look beautiful tonight.' Then he resumed back to his silent treatment of her, killing the very joy she'd experienced by the compliment.

They later went over to the buffet table where waiters were serving hot curried goat and rice, and took their pick of the sub-continental salad. Jace still remained stoney silent with such obvious discourtesy, it bordered on criminal intent.

Finally, with a small frown drawing her well marked brows together, Tammy said with an iota of detachment, 'You could at least make an effort to be nice.' When he failed to answer, she went on. 'I've had to deal with all the questions regarding our so called marriage.' Still Jace said nothing. Tammy glanced at him. His dark profile was grim and set, his eyes frosting over like glaciers and suddenly the words tumbled out in a rush. 'Do you really hate me that much?' She was furious, but she held her voice low as to remain inconspicious.

'I'm sure my co-operation isn't a pre-requisite to our marriage,' he said plainly, his tone holding a faint tint of menace, as though concealing some kind of threat. 'You've made it perfectly obvious that you don't want me to touch you. Your coldhearted little scheme proved that quite clearly.'

Tammy's nerves rippled like the surface of a pool icing over. 'Spare me the lecture on my scruples,' she boomed. 'I'm going to powder my nose.' She marched away as quickly as she could, fighting down the tension in her chest that suddenly became unbearably stifling. She needed some solitude, a few minutes of respite from Jace's chilling presence.

The ladies room was lavishly furnished with an en-suite dressing room adjacent the entrance door that featured a whole wall completely made up of mirrors. Tammy sank into one of the padded dralon chairs and opened her handbag in search of her face powder. Dabbing the soft translucent flakes to her face to dampen the evening's prespiration, she planned a strategy on how she would handle Jace.

The aloof impersonal formality bit wasn't working, simply because Jace was already applying that tactic himself, she sighed, deciding on adding a little blusher to replace the glow back into her peeky cheeks. Maybe if she were to ignore him, as he was ignoring her, then it could throw him of guard, she thought. No, that wouldn't work either, Tammy shrugged defeated. Jace's wit would detect that play in an instant.

She plucked nervously at strands of her hair then smoothed them back into place. Her only recourse was to go on acting the devoted, upstanding bride-to-be and take Jace's smiling disregard with a pinch of salt in the process. Closing her bag, Tammy rose from the dressing table preparatory to leaving, but as she did so, she was suddenly aware that she was not alone. Sherelle had followed her in.

'It wouldn't be nice of me to come in here without congratulating you personally,' Sherelle said, forcing a smile to her hard, delectible features.

'On my marriage?' Tammy answered with naivety, turning to face the woman, yet undetecting Sherelle's hint at irony.

'Oh no,' the singer spoke with spite. 'On your cleverness.'

Tammy's eyes widened. 'Sorry?'

'You're a thousand times smarter than I'd have given you credit for,' Sherelle confirmed coldly. 'You see, I know about your little game even if you think that I don't and I have to admit that you've won tonight's round decisively.'

'I didn't know that we were contesting,' Tammy spoke back, sarcasm rising to her aid.

Sherelle laughed harshly. 'But of course we are. Girl, I can admit it because I'm an experienced campaigner. It's obvious that you haven't the gall to admit that we're at battle and *we are* both out for Jace aren't we?'

'I'm sure Jace will give a war medal to the victor,' Tammy quipped with scorn. 'I sincerely hope that you're the one who receives it.'

Sherelle stepped back, disguising her surprise well as she watched Tammy almost glide right by her. 'Don't antagonise Jace when the marriage is over,' she raised her voice to carry her words over to Tammy whose hand was now braced on the gold doorknob. 'Just get the divorce settlement when you can.'

Tammy made her way back into the large room, struggling with the sudden tears which threatened. It was just like Jace to get mixed up with a primetime bitch, she thought treacherously. Sherelle Tate had to be at the top of the heap.

Jace was socializing from across the vast room when he raised his head above the web of humanity in search of her. His brown eyes immediately met Tammy's with a perceptual sense of sudden understanding and in a matter of seconds, he was quickly making his way over to her, almost abruptly pushing over two elderly women in his progress. 'What's the matter?' he queried with a genuine ebb to his voice on finally reaching her.

'Nothing,' Tammy replied.

Jace seized her wrist and gently pulled her to a discreet corner of the room. 'I saw Sherelle follow you. Has she been . . .'

'I don't want to talk about it,' Tammy interrupted, composing herself quickly and pulling her wrist away from Jace. 'I've had enough of you, of everybody. You can all go to hell.'

'Tammy?'   Jace's hands slid up her arm to her shoulders, then tightened, moving her an inch closer to him. Tammy snapped her head up, intending to tell Jace to get lost, but his lips instantly captured her attention. Jace's response was instantly obliging as he dipped his head and covered her mouth with his.

The kiss had been the briefest of kisses, only a brush across her lips, first in one direction and then the other, but it was enough to cause an explosion inside Tammy that forced her body to arch against Jace's and her hands to tremble uncontrollably.

'Are you alright now?' Jace asked softly as he gently released her, his free hand sliding up and down her spine in a lazy caress.

Tammy nodded dumbfounded.

Jace backed away steadily. 'That's just for the benefit of everyone here,' he added firmly, rejecting the sudden unfamiliar emotion budding deep inside him. 'I'll not infringe upon your affections.'

Tammy opened her mouth, the words stringing in her head ready to tell Jace that she very much wanted to grant him the rights to her body and to her affections, when Calvin miraculousy appeared from nowhere, aborted her attempt at making amends and pulled her madly toward him. 'I demand you to take your dirty rotten, two-timing hands of my sis,' he told Jace with fury. 'You're really something you know that? You're really a piece of work to think you can have it all, obligating yourself to two women. Well not my sis.'

'Calvin!' Tammy raised her voice, alarmed.

'Don't you dare side with that rat,' Calvin warned. 'You're just an innocent little virgin who needs protecting against bastards like him.'

Tammy jerked her arm away and wrapped it around her stomach, moving sideways to escape the sensationally shocked expression featured comically across Jace's face.

'She's a what?' she heard him gasp, his voice weak with raw amazement.

'A virgin,' Calvin confirmed angrily. 'And if you lay a finger on her again, I'll bust . . . '

'Why don't you yell a little louder?' Tammy almost screamed at her brother. 'There's a guy in Africa who didn't quite hear you.'

Jace caught her by the arms, but she broke free and ran toward the emergency exit, almost falling over her dress as she pushed the door open and felt the cool night breeze ripple her velvet garment. Jace followed in hot pursuit, catching up with her at the rear end of the building.

'Leave me alone,' Tammy cried tearfully too blinded by her own torment to see the tortured regret that darkened Jace's brown eyes.

'It's not the end of the world,' Jace told her, the guilt tinged in his voice.

'It will be for you if you don't leave me alone,' Tammy yelled back, lifting her handbag in an incensed threat.

Jace's gaze shifted to her raised hand. 'Go ahead,' he coaxed. 'I deserve it, teasing you over something you obviously know nothing about.'

'Oh, I get it,' Tammy said with an ache in her voice as her gaze riveted on the tall, solemn man standing a foot away from her. 'We virgins aren't supposed to know what making love is all about right?'

'Making love isn't just a sexual thing,' Jace clarified softly. 'It's a union of two people. Companionship, loyalty, commitment . . .'

'That's a laugh,' Tammy interrupted hysterically, attempting to sidle away from him. 'I thought they called that a marriage. Fat chance of me attaining that with you.'

'You're upset,' Jace said, stepping into her path, reaching out to stop her escaping from him.

'I'm not upset,' Tammy yelled back stubbornly. She tried to run, but her legs were shaking with emotion to do anything, let alone move from the spot where she was rooted. Instead, she fell helpless into Jace's opened arms and sobbed quietly to herself.

She sobbed for Calvin's outrageous outburst, for her naivety with Sherelle, for her weakness to stand up firmly against Jace, and most of all, for her grandmother's latest attack and the assimilation she had to uphold with Jace to maintain Hattie's stability. A time went by until her tears were totally spent. Fighting back the exquisite beauty of being in Jace's arms, of being pressed against his tall, strong body, Tammy gently pushed herself free.

She wiped the remaining tears with the back of her hand and rose her forlorn gaze to Jace's face. 'Can I go now?'

Jace was relunctant to release her. 'Why didn't you tell me?' he demanded softly. 'It would've become self-evident to me sooner or later.'

'Before or after you got me into the marital bed?' Tammy scoffed with a hiccough.

'And what if my arms were where you ultimately end up, as my wife?' Jace prodded, unashamed at his suggestion of their bodies being locked in an intimate union. 'At this rate, I'd say that our wedding was right on schedule with a honeymoon to follow, in my bed!'

Tammy's face flushed with renewed shame. 'I'd sooner become a nun than share your bed.'

Jace's face hardened, though his voice remained solaced and warm. 'Come on.' He caught her hand, twisting his wrist to lace his fingers through hers.

'Where are we going?' Tammy quipped, giddily aware of his strong, warm fingers clasping hers.

'I'm taking you home,' Jace declared. 'You're obviously not in any fit state to see the night through, and I don't want to risk a scandal for your grandmother's sake with so many press photographers around.'

'But I've left my cape at the coats' desk,' Tammy protested.

'I'll arrange for someone to bring it over,' Jace affirmed.

SILENCE CLOSED around them once again on the ride home. Tammy welcomed the cool night air breezing through the open car window, lightly teasing the straying wisps of her thick black hair.

She forced herself to think logically. She had two

immediate problems facing her; the first was that it was now obvious Jace intended that if they were forced to marry, he would take her to his bed. In his mind's eye, that was already a foregone conclusion. Of course, she could skip the country or still try to persuade her grandmother that she could wait, forever if need be, but her second problem was that she wasn't at all certain if that was what she wanted.

Jace was a difficult person to come to grasps with. One minute he'd be steely formal, the next passionately masculine. Maybe she brought out the worse in him; maybe he wasn't normally so inconsistent. Tammy couldn't decide. Such a personality instability had to mean something though.

She wondered what Jace was thinking and turned to study his side profile. She could tell he was contemplating the traffic and concentrating on some other matter at the same time. He was probably deciding on how to treat her, Tammy thought scornfully. His newly acclaimed knowledge of her private virtue would obviously now command a degree of his respect and maybe a dose of good manners too. That was already becoming apparent, but it only served in enhancing her attraction toward him all the more.

She should be taking great delight in reminding him of his indiscriminate past. The elation of having one over on Jace Washington should be rendering her estatic. Surely there was nothing more ironic, on his part, than to find that he was in the wrong all along and the very person he'd tried to smudge was infact purified of all stain.

Yet, although the disclosure may've left her widely embarrassed and allowed her to witness the expression of total disbelief on Jace's face, a sudden relief also washed over Tammy. A relief she felt certain she should reject for it brought out her vulnerability and that in turn could dangerously lead toward total self-betrayal.

When they arrived outside her front door, Tammy eyed

Jace nervously, her mind wondering if he was going to leave immediately, her fingers fidgeting with the door key as she also contemplated whether he intended on kissing her again.

His firm clipped voice soon attested to his intentions. 'I want a word with you if you'd like to invite me in.'

Tammy warily judged his determined stance and raised cautious brows. 'Well I . . .'

'I'm not planning on staying longer than five minutes,' Jace jeered, 'so you can safely rule out rape.'

Tammy's face burned as she opened the door and switched on the lights. For a moment, she felt like a complete idiot for hesitating with the very man who'd kissed her until the world had spun on its axis.

Quickly fighting her composure, she led the way into the sitting room and turned on the lights there before proceeding to turn on the electric heater. 'I - I can offer you some coffee if you like,' she invited by way of a token apology for her hesitation earlier.

'I take mine black, two sugars,' Jace accepted. 'And,' he gripped her wrist lightly, restraining her from leaving right away. 'I'm sorry for the way I behaved earlier, especially tonight. If I'd known . . .'

'I accept your apology,' Tammy interrupted, anxious to steer clear of the subject. 'The damage was only done to my pride, not my virtue.'

Jace studied her with curious eyes. 'You forgive me then?'

'You said you were sorry.'

'And I am, really.'

Tammy waved a dismissing hand. 'I'll go and get the coffee.'

She disappeared into the kitchen and arrived back a few minutes later with two steaming cups of coffee. Jace had seated himself comfortably in one of the white leather chairs encircling the brightly lit fireplace, his right ankle raised above his left knee.

He'd spotted the family album she often kept lying about freely on top of the television and had taken it up, flicking slowly through the pages. Tammy felt a little self-conscious as she desposited the two cups on the slate black coffee table.

Jace's head shot up and a weak, tied smile crossed his face. 'Thanks. Is this you?' He was pointing at a picture of her when she was five years old, her hair braided tightly into small plaits and dressed in a pink floral pinafore that had once been her favourite.

'Yes,' Tammy smiled in reminiscence. 'That was taken on my first day at school.'

'Cute,' Jace said warmly. 'And I hadn't realised until now that you still have your childhood dimple.'

Tammy's heart warmed. 'My mother always told me it wouldn't go away.'

'Which one is your mother?'

Tammy's smile faded as her eyes rested on the small photograph she spied from the top corner of the album. Seating herself next to Jace, she pointed at the vertical mono snapshot.

'There.' Her index finger inadvertently began to trace the age lines left by sticky tape. 'I haven't looked at that picture in over a year,' she admitted. 'Sometimes, it's still so painful.'

'I know about your parents,' Jace declared with sympathy. 'Your mother looked just like you. Is this your father?'

Tammy nodded and again traced the lines embedded into the photograph, recalling her fondest moments of early life.

An hour passed quickly. She'd shown Jace almost every snapshot in the album. Her first kitten, Calvin's hamster. Their trip to the seaside when she was eight; a visit to London zoo. Her whole life seemed chronicled in the 24 page album from the first photograph of her aged five to the holiday snap of her in a yellow bikini which Calvin had taken a year ago in Barbados.

She'd learned a little about Jace too. It was the opening Tammy so desperately wanted. He was born to Afro-Brazilian parents who'd raised him by struggling to scrape two pennies together amidst the poverty that had gripped the country. His impoverished childhood had made him strong and determined and he'd been lucky to receive a scholarship to further his education. Her grandmother had played a part too, regularly sending cheques to cover exam and accommodation expenses throughout his college education in America.

Despite his upbringing - no, in spite of it, Jace had become a ruthless, independent businessman and was the pride of his parents who'd mercifully lived through their hardship to share in the wealth he'd built. His father now actively took part in the day to day running of his operations, re-educating himself with the advancements of modern technology, and his mother was actively engaged in charities that fought for the prevention and reduction of violence against street-wise children.

Finally Jace closed the photo album and rubbed his tied eyes. His coffee cup was almost drained and the sleep lines were evident in his face, drawing at the taut set of his brows. 'Before I go,' he yawned discreetly, merging his fingers together with elbows braced against his knees. 'I think you ought to know that my parents are arriving from Brazil tomorrow.' He sighed. 'They're expecting to meet you, so I told them you'd have some time on Sunday.'

'This is all very sudden,' Tammy said weakly, the surprise numbing her shock. 'I mean, a week hasn't passed yet and already you're arranging that I be introduced to the prospective in-laws.' Her rage caught up with the shock. 'Just exactly what did you tell your parents?'

'I told them that they may read or hear about my engagement to you,' Jace chided, his tone tinged with the same annoyance. 'And I told my mother not to take it seriously, but ...'

'She still decided she'd like to meet me,' Tammy interrupted rudely. She rose from her seat and rubbed a tied finger against her forehead. 'This is getting out of hand,' she rattled, pacing the floor. 'I knew I shouldn't have gone along with this - this hair-raising plan of yours. What do we do now?'

Jace rose from his seat. 'Do whatever you want,' he quipped impatiently. 'I'm too tied to think let alone argue.' He made toward the door. 'I'll see you in the morning.'

'You're going to drive home like that?' Tammy asked suddenly alarmed, the concern reflecting in her eyes.

'Like what?'

'Like that! Too tied to see straight.'

'I can hardly share your bed,' Jace mocked. 'Think of your virtue against an unscrupulous womanizer like me.'

'I have a spare room,' Tammy flinched. 'I can't promise you a shaving stick and razor, but you'll find the bed comfortable. And before you tease,' she added, 'I can sleep with the knowledge that you'll be yards away from my bed, however misguided you think I am.'

Jace folded his arms against his chest and gazed intently at her face, his eyes appraising every feminine curve concealed provocatively beneath her red velvet dress. 'Just out of curiosity,' he queried, puzzled, dubious and distinctly probing. 'What in the hell are you waiting for?'

'I don't know what you mean,' Tammy answered evasively.

'Try again,' Jace smiled wickedly, stifling a yawn.

'I haven't met the right man,' Tammy mumbled uneasily. 'I'll go and see if there are any clean sheets on that spare bed.'

Jace followed her into the medium-sized corner bedroom that was elaborately furnished and housed a four poster bed. 'Do you think you've met the right man now?' he edged in genuine bemusement, leaning against the door frame, charting her expression.

Tammy flinched inwardly. She knew Jace was referring to himself and she also knew that her attraction toward him was growing stronger by the second, but she felt compelled not to admit to it, at least not whilst he was sharing her apartment for the night.

'I'm still searching,' she answered, not daring to look at him.

Jace's amused brown eyes flickered down to her level. 'I see. So I'm not in the running then?' he countered with a twist of his lips.

Tammy busied herself with smoothing the duvet, her heart beginning to pound loudly against her chest. 'These are fresh sheets, so you should sleep comfortably,' she steered.

'I'd sleep better next to you,' Jace coaxed.

'I don't think I like being equated with a sleeping pill,' Tammy said shakily, lamely suppressing the shooting sparks of desire racing wildly through her body.

'Who's talking about sleeping?' Jace remarked cheekily. 'You can *put* me to sleep.'

'No I couldn't,' Tammy evaded, her head dizzy with the rush of heat spurned on by Jace's suggestive banter.

'Shall I come over there and prove it?'

'No,' Tammy panicked, edging back two steps. In her haste, she clumsily caught her knees on the side of the bed, lost her balance and fell flat on her back on the duvet covered mattress.

'Can't wait?' Jace laughed heartily, slowly advancing the distance from the door toward her.

Tammy looked at his strong capable hands and reflected wistfully on his masculine fingers tracing the contours of her body, exciting her into submission. She shifted uneasily on the bed for she'd never before in her life wanted a man to make love to her as much as she wanted Jace Washington.

CHAPTER SIX

JACE COVERED Tammy's hand with his large warm one, squeezing her fingers gently as he helped her to her feet. Tammy had never felt so embarrassed in all her life. To land flat on her back on the very bed she was to loan Jace for the night and to want him as badly as she did had rendered her speechless.

'You're behaving a little premature,' Jace joked, staring down at her, a wealth of unreadable expressions drawn across his face. 'I thought you'd save that until after the wedding.'

Swift heat coarsed along Tammy's body. 'Must you read something intimate into everything I say or do?' she temporized, desperately trying to quell the hurry of her pulsebeats.

'I can't help it when I'm with you,' Jace grinned impishly, deliberately casting hazy brown eyes over the alluring curves of her enticing figure.

'Goodnight Jace,' Tammy said firmly. 'I guess you don't need me in here for anything else.'

Jace's hands tightened around her fingers, relunctant to let her go. 'Do you toss out provocative remarks like that on purpose,' he said hoarsely, regarding her with an enigmatic, hopeful gaze, 'or am I right in thinking that you want me as much as I want you?'

This was getting out of hand, Tammy decided, unable to fight the little flames in Jace's eyes that seemed to scorch her. She should be thinking up an excuse to leave, or at least be edging her way toward the door for a quick exit. Getting intimate with Jace could only mean one thing, giving up on her old fashioned values and accepting the need to be loved and be in love. Yet, that was what she wanted. It felt right, it seemed right too.

Jace cupped Tammy's chin in his palm, raising her face to his. He detected the strength of her heartbeats racing wildly against her chest and observed the amorous look of longing in her hazel eyes that reflected his own. Accepting her silence by way of consent, he slowly dipped his head and tentatively sought her lips, capturing them in a series of slow, tempting mouthfuls.

Never before in her life had Tammy felt such a need to be fulfilled, to be passionately embraced in Jace's arms forever. With a fervent need to feel him closer, she clung tightly to his waist, drugged by the force of his tongue exploring the inner depth of her mouth.

The world tilted sideways as Jace eased her back down on to the bed, his free hand deftly unzipping the red velvet dress that clad her warm, trembling body. Within seconds, he had undressed her and was already in search of the tiny clip that fastened her bra from behind.

Tammy heard him groan with delight as the lace and silk bra slipped helpless to the foot of the bed. She heard her own alien groan in response and marvelled at her self-determined revelation as his tongue encircled an exposed nipple and sucked it ardently. She was slipping fast and deep into Jace's ocean of desire.

Guided only by instinct, her fingers began to move of their own volition, removing Jace's tie and then his tuxedo and white ruffled shirt. She drew a laboured breath as Jace's manly cinnamon chest was revealed to her inexperienced eyes. He was so virile and muscular, she thought, so intoxicated with the knowledge that he was also hers to touch, that Tammy scarcely noticed when he had removed her lace panties from beneath her, or his own underpants.

Suddenly all the arguments against their pretense relationship, which she knew to be valid, fled into the darkness of the night. The fact that she'd told Jace she would physically resist him, that she had no wish to be seduced and that she was not impressed by his masculinity, all dissolved with every brush of his lips. Lips that explored every part of her body and fanned the slow fire that burned within her into a roaring inferno of hot scorching passion.

At that point, nothing mattered. Not the company, not Calvin's inheritance, not even Sherelle's bitchiness. Only Hattie's peace of mind over her engagement to Jace momentarily prevailed and Tammy was already inadvertently honouring that commitment. Jace's lips washed away all her doubts and promised a night of ultimate ecstasy as he swept her into his arms.

He shifted on top of her and something wild and fierce stirred within Tammy, ready to welcome him. Yet the moment Jace's knees began to wedge their way between her legs, Tammy's entire body jerked into rigid, involuntary alarm.

'Jace wait,' she gasped, clamping her legs together, stunning the very sparkle that had ignited between them. 'I haven't . . .'

'Tammy, don't,' Jace commanded with a raw ache in his voice, overruling her refusal of him stoically. 'Just relax,' he coaxed in a whisper as he nuzzled kisses against her neck. 'Let it happen.'

'But I . . .' Tammy was about to tell him that she hadn't any contraceptives when Jace's next words knocked her for six.

'I'm going to be your husband in a few weeks,' he interrupted persuasively. 'So let's exercise some prudence and get this over with.'

Tammy descended from the misty euphoria from where she was floating, sated and happy, her boneless contentment suddenly giving way to harsh reality.

Jace didn't care for her one iota. Deep down, he probably didn't even like her. The thought of taking her to bed, however, was an enticing prospect on his part and that distinct possibility was enough to creep into her fogged mind and disturb the bliss of the moment.

She suddenly recalled how he'd told her that her very domane was pledged to him, that he would succeed in taming her to submit to his demands and that he hadn't gone far enough, but intended to. It was all falling into place, despite her virtue as a virgin. Jace had expected to sample the goods and she was innocently helping him do it. His words only served in confirming that suspicion.

'Get this over with,' she repeated, appalled at his use of phrase. 'Is that all I am to you, a frivolous sex object that you want to try out?'

'I didn't mean it like that,' Jace conceded, planting a kiss on the tip of her nose.

'How did you mean it?'

Jace sighed, disliking the conversation, his face evident that he wanted nothing more than to get right back to where they'd left of. 'Listen,' he reasoned. 'I'm not stealing anything that doesn't already rightly belong to me. I just thought ...'

'Tell me,' Tammy interrupted uneasily. 'When you discovered that I was a virgin tonight, did you have any reservations at all about taking me to bed or were you just more determined that we made love?'

Jace looked at her levelly. 'The truth?'

Tammy nodded.

'More determined.'

Tammy was still reeling from the blow of those two words when Jace dipped his head and began to trace kisses down the centre of her breasts to her navel.

'Jace.' She wriggled onto her side, the alarm etched in her face. 'Why were you more determined?'

'What difference does it make?' Jace countered, raising his head.

Tammy rolled away from him and hastily sat up, reaching for his discarded shirt at the foot of the bed.

'What are you doing?' Jace demanded, watching Tammy plunge her arms into his sleeves to conceal her nakedness.

'I'm going to my room,' Tammy answered obstinately.

'Dammit!' Jace reached for his underpants and quickly slipped into them. 'What do you want me to say? I want you.'

'What you want is to get me into bed before either one of us can say Rio Negro,' Tammy flared. 'The fact that I'm a virgin just makes it more of a challenge for you. How could I have been so stupid as to think that you might actually care about me.'

Jace's jaw tightened. 'Don't be such a prude,' he jabbed. 'Just because you're a virgin doesn't change my views about you. I just thought a little practice before the wedding would eliminate the honeymoon from being a total washout.'

Tammy's blood ran cold. She felt transparent, weak and ill all at the same time. It was obvious Jace saw her inhibited sexuality as an imposing and threatening problem for him. How dare he even regard her that way, as though she'd been bargained over and was now being taught the proper premliminaries for intimate married life.

When she finally spoke, her voice was trembling with emotion. 'If anything's a washout, it's you and everything you stand for. We don't love each other and therefore I don't see why we should go to bed together, neither before or after the wedding should it come to that.'

She marched toward the door, but Jace caught up with her and gripped her arm tightly. 'I'll not be denied my marital rights,' he raged. 'If we are forced to marry, I'll do my dammest to consummate it.'

'I'd rather fumble in the dark with a man as naive as myself than with the official Brazilian contender to the bedroom olympics.'

'Fine,' Jace spat back, releasing her. 'If that's the kind of wimp you want for a husband, that's fine by me. I can probably give him a few pointers on where to start, like with that holier than thou, uppercrust and stuck up manner of yours.'

Tammy's face hardened. 'I wondered when we were going to get round to discussing personalities,' she boomed knowingly. 'I told Calvin once that I personally found your manners intolerable, but I take that all back. Aside from your infidelity, intolerable isn't descriptive enough of the repugnant cynical behaviour and impertinence that you possess. You're the worse person I've ever had the misfortune to meet.'

Jace flinched, but his eyes remained coldly fixed and his voice lowered to a deadly tone. 'You'd better go to your room before that strait-laced, guileless facade of yours fail to withstand indecent language.'

Tammy saw the murderous trait in his face and knew Jace meant every word he said. She wasted no time in seeking the haven of her own bedroom, leaning against her pine-style door as though she was forcefully shutting out the angry contempt that had flared between them.

She felt vulnerable, afraid and a touch inadequate. Jace had wanted her tonight and she had badly wanted him, but not at the expense of submitting to his well planned demands which he'd intended on executing with such timely precision.

That had disappointed her. She'd felt her virginity would've stood for something. Maybe eliciting a little pride from Jace that his wife-to-be was untouched, or that he was honoured to be the first to have swept away the barriers of protection and self-preservation she'd built up all these years. But instead, Jace had targeted her inhibition by making the whole thing out to be a preliminary act before the nuptials, deriding her very virtue in the process.

Little did he know that her fear of sexual intimacy was a fear of her own lack of experience. Yet with Jace, Tammy felt no fear, no hesitation, nothing that could've taken away the frantic excitement she'd found so overwhelming. So why hadn't Jace picked up on that?

Tammy weakly unbuckled the clasp that held in place the choker around her neck. Jace probably found her tiresome in comparison to the experienced women he was famely accustomed. Sherelle Tate was such a woman; pretty, ambitious, self-confident and knowing exactly how to please a man.

Releasing the pearl droplets from her ears, she knew that Jace probably wished he'd left the charity gala with Sherelle. The thought made her tense. Sherelle intended on getting Jace back and had the right qualities to do it. After tonight, Jace could easily be susceptible to change and that in turn could be disasterous news to her grandmother's state of mind and health.

Tammy walked over to her jewel box and deposited the choker and earrings. If she wanted to keep Jace and uphold her part of their arrangement, she'd have to submit to him. That meant going along with the wedding plans and sharing his bed. It was a proposal she felt bound to contemplate for she knew that despite the rapid hiccoughs that seemed ever to frequent their relationship, she was also irrevocably falling in love.

TAMMY FLINCHED her eyes as the early morning sun forced its way through her bedroom curtains. Frowning, she tossed onto her side, assessed the time from the bedside clock, then rolled onto her back.

It was 9.30 am. She had stayed awake for most of the night until the sky had started to pale, only giving in to sleep sometime around six o'clock. Now, the toils of the night felt heavy against her eyelids and she relunctantly crawled from beneath the cotton sheets and made her way over to the en-suite bathroom.

She expelled a groan as she caught sight of herself in the bathroom mirror. It reflected the ravages Jace had wrought the night before and showed the frustration that rose above the circles beneath her eyes.

Pulling a grimace at her wretched expression, Tammy sighed wearily and turned on the shower. Standing beneath the hot steaming downpour of water, she was able to vent away some of the anguish that fogged her mind over seeing Jace that morning.

She wondered what he ate for breakfast, then scoffed over the idea at having to prepare it for him. Her mind lingered on whether he'd bring up the topic of last night, then reeled over the fact that he was to blame for it all. She contemplated his stance, and treacherously decided he'd behave the way he always did, coldly cynical. Just thinking about him stimulated such a traumatic sensation that by the time she left the shower cubicle, her head had acquired a throbbing pain.

Donning a pink towel as the only means of concealing her body, Tammy went in search of the box of paracetamols she normally kept in a cabinet above the kitchen sink.

She hadn't expected Jace to be awake, especially after the contentious kind of night they had both had, but the moment she walked boldly into the kitchen, her body froze with acute surprise. Jace was stood over the kitchen hob, flagged only in a lime green towel around his waist and frying up plantain and eggs whilst humming to a Michael Jackson tune bellowing low from her portable stereo player.

Tammy sucked in her breath as she observed his muscular semi-naked frame which appeared more built up and bronzed in the morning daylight, his tapering torso and long, hairy legs perfectly sculpted. His wet hair was a glistening shade of jet black, indicative that he too had taken a shower and his jaw sported the shadow of a stubborn beard. She desperately tried not to react to the epitome of an African god standing before her by choosing instead to hint at when Jace was planning to leave her premises.

'I thought you'd gone already,' she lied nervously,

clinging at the soft towel that hid her quavering limbs.

'You're not going to begrudge me breakfast?' Jace queried stiffly, diverting his attention to cast his icy gaze upon her. When she didn't offer him an answer, he added coldly, 'I called about your cape earlier and the hotel is going to arrange to have it sent over.'

Tammy considered thanking him, then relented on the thought that it was all his fault why it had been left there in the first place.

'And by the way,' she heard him add in a tone that immediately called for her special attention. 'Calvin phoned.'

'Calvin phoned?' Tammy repeated, annoyed at herself for having turned off the telephone in her bedroom so she would not be disturbed if she'd happened to succeed in getting some sleep. 'What did he want?'

'Well in the first instance,' Jace said bluntly, tossing the plantain with a fork, 'he wanted to know why I was here and where you were. I told him that you were still in bed and that I'd stayed the night. I think we can safely plan to expect him round here at any minute.'

'What!'

'Depending on how long it'll take Sherelle Tate to leave his bed.'

Tammy's mouth dried out. 'Calvin and Sherelle are . . .'

'Soulmates by now,' Jace interrupted casually, too casual for Tammy's comfort. 'Which is more than I can say for us,' he added sarcastically. 'How do you take your eggs?'

Tammy peered at him, the frustration of a new day of conflict beginning to build on her until it seeped to the surface. Deciding to stay on the subject of her brother though, she quipped, 'I don't believe that's possible. Calvin wouldn't . . .'

'Calvin isn't a wide eyed innocent like you,' Jace jabbed, 'so spare me the song and dance about his monogamy. It doesn't exist.'

'And neither does yours,' Tammy chided, conceding to the fact that she may not rightfully be able to protect her brother on the strength of his past, but she could tactfully remind Jace of his by way of defence. 'You deliberately gave Calvin misleading information about us.'

'I told him the truth,' Jace countered, his voice tinged with annoyance.

'You told him everything and nothing,' Tammy returned with the same annoyance. 'Well I'm glad he's scored a point by stealing your lover right from under you. I can't say that I'm amazed it doesn't seem to have bothered you too much.'

Jace ignored her remark and continued aloud, 'I guess you don't take your eggs sunny-side-up. Shall I hard boil them to remain consistent with your present mood?'

Tammy leaned against the kitchen sink, a lump forming against her throat as she tried to dispel the effect Jace's impassive behaviour was having on her. 'I like my eggs well done,' she intoned, folding her arms stubbornly beneath her breasts.

Jace's lips twitched as he cracked two eggs to join the other three in the frying pan, preciding over them with the same scrutiny of a gourmet chef. Without lifting his head he said stoically, 'You haven't made any secret of the fact that you resent the way I've forced myself into your life, so why are you worrying yourself over how I feel about Sherelle?'

'Like you, I don't have any feelings about Sherelle one way or the other,' Tammy remarked firmly. 'I don't even rate her music, so you can scrap the theory about me being jealous.'

'Johnnie cakes?' Jace queried lightly, in total disregard of her statement.

Tammy stared up at him, pinched with the knowledge that their conversation wasn't affecting him in the slightest, certainly not in the way she expected it would. 'Two,' she answered tightly, casting her eyes over the plate of fried dumplings he'd obviously prepared earlier.

She watched him as he turned the eggs, admiring his tapered body from behind, then inwardly frowned over her stupidity. If anything was to teach her how informally involved Jace was with his female acquaintances, it had to be the revelation of Sherelle's affair with her brother. He just didn't care.

She was surprised however, that Sherelle's allegiance could be so easily entrusted to another man. That, she felt, needed an explanation and her heart momentarily soared when Jace suddenly provided her with the answer she required.

'Sherelle was a miscalculation of judgement,' he told her repressively. 'I dated her because I wanted her to be seen with me publicly. I wanted the press to misconstrue her media endorsement of my new range of protein conditioning hair relaxers which I launched recently at the Afro Hair and Beauty Exhibition here in London.'

'Why her?' Tammy asked blithely.

'Damned if I know,' Jace exclaimed, transferring the contents of the frying pan into two plates he'd positioned on the breakfast table. 'Because she's got a good head of hair maybe.'

'It's probably a wig or extensions,' Tammy mocked jealously.

He returned the pan to the hob then enquired, 'Where do you keep the salt?'

Tammy pointed at the cabinet above her head where she'd decided to come in search of paracetamols earlier. Eleviating her headache was the last thing on her mind though as she watched Jace obliterate the distance between them, his body coming precariously within centrimetres of her so that she could physically feel the impact of his manhood beneath the towelling around his waist pressing against her.

A flame of fire bolted right through her entire nervous system, causing her to feel dizzy and light headed. To her chagrin, she reacted to the intense heat by arching against him in a fevered need to know again the overwhelming sensation that had sparked between them the night before.

Jace's mobile lips smiled knowingly, obviously aware of his effect on her. Retrieving the salt, he placed it on the sink top behind her then returned his hand and tipped Tammy's chin to meet the glow of elation spread wildly across his face. 'Incase you're wondering,' he whispered against her trembling lips. 'I haven't slept with Sherelle.'

Tammy's body crumbled into a thousand pieces with a combination of joy over the news that Sherelle hadn't been Jace's lover, and the burning desire to be kissed. She suddenly wanted to make up for the defiance that had erupted between them, to surrender to the pull of him which was so strong and ease the tension that had built up between them over the past few days.

Tilting her head, she closed her eyes and waited impatiently for the feel of Jace's lips to meet hers. Instead, it was his voice that bounced against her cheeks, his tone deliberately obvious that he was not intending to oblige her silent demand. 'Have you any mango chutney?' he asked flatly.

Tammy opened her eyes, just as Jace released her chin, her mind consciously aware that he had no interest in kissing her. Nodding her head, she leaned against the sink, bewildered by his attitude, more by the fact that he'd rejected her, but she was utterly stunned by his next words.

'I'm not in any desperate hurry to make love to you,' he informed her crudely. 'So I'd say your timing was a bit off.'

'My timing?' Tammy almost choked over her words and on Jace's outrageous presumption that she was the one doing the chasing and not him. 'It's your sense of proportion that's a bit bent,' she raged. 'I wasn't the one tempting cupid last night.'

'And I wasn't alone when cupid was being tempted,' Jace fired back.

Tammy flinched recalling the scene of the night before.

With a regal inclination of her head to disguise the churning mass of vulnerability, humiliation and shattered illusions, she said, 'I'm going to go and change.'

Jace's throaty chuckle followed her as she left the kitchen, grating against her ragged nerves like the effect of sandpaper.

She'd be damned if she was going to display any weakness now. Certainly the strain of the last few days was enough to hack at anyone's senses, assuming anyone had a grandmother who was ill, a brother whose very future was being threatened and a marriage looming over their head to a person they almost despised.

It was time she considered pulling herself together and attempt to rectify the situation, she thought wryly. Calvin's ideas were far too unethical and so were some of her earlier schemes. Handling Jace Washington called for a special kind of ground rule. Tammy was already mentally rehearsing one that instantly sprung to mind.

Pulling on a pair of designer jeans and a white motifed sweater, she vigrously dried her hair, applied some activator, then displayed it wildly to fit her mood, allowing the soft wetlook curls to spill over her shoulders in deep, swirling waves.

She decided on applying only a hint of makeup and gold scalloped earrings to exact a shade of sophistication. Picking up Jace's ruffled shirt which she'd slung over her cane bedroom chair the night before, Tammy marched defiantly into the sitting room, her mind alert and her scattered wits in place.

Jace was sat at the regency style dinner table at the far end of the room, where he'd placed their breakfasts, his mind absorbed in the task of pulling on woollen socks. He was practically dressed with the exception of his shirt and his tie hung redundant around his neck.

'Your shirt,' Tammy said tightly, tossing it across the room toward him. Jace caught it unerringly then eyed her with suspicion. 'If you want it ironed,' she added coldly, 'you'll have to do that yourself.'

Jace laughed. 'I can see the aftermath of our marriage is not going to bear heavily on your household chores.'

'You know what you can do about that,' Tammy retorted.

'Buy an iron?' Jace joked, putting on his shirt.

Tammy was not amused.

'Listen,' Jace intoned gently. 'I have alot to do today. I have to go home, shave, change and be at the airport in less than an hour, so can I suggest that we eat breakfast on mutual territory, preferably with no concealed weapons?'

Tammy shrugged. 'If you wish.'

Breakfast was eaten in relative silence, Jace devouring the eggs, plantain and johnnie cakes in a matter of minutes, then drinking a glass of orange, followed by tea to wash down the salty taste on his tongue.

Tammy wanted to compliment him on the fried dumplings which she found fairly appetising, but knew Jace would only see that as her way of apologising, so she instead ate them without comment.

That didn't stop Jace, however, from prompting a response. 'Breakfast okay?' he queried curiously, watching as she placed her used fork on the empty plate.

'Let's just say you'd probably make someone a good husband,' Tammy said begrudgingly.

'I intend to make you an ideal husband if you'll let me,' Jace clarified, 'which reminds me. I'm picking up the marriage licence on Monday.'

Tammy tensed, then quickly composed herself, remembering her sudden decision earlier that morning. 'There's just one other provision then,' she said sweetly, knowing that what she was about to say would infuriate Jace past reason.

Jace's brows rose. 'What's that?'

'The pre-nuptial agreement.'

Jace evidently lost his tongue, his expression warred with amazement. It was an age before he spoke. 'What in the hell are you talking about?'

'Now don't behave so shocked,' Tammy reasoned, enjoying the anger she'd evoked in him. 'It's only a simple contractual arrangement.'

'You make me sound like a business merger,' Jace's voice held steel. 'There's nothing in the world you want that I can't buy so I don't understand what you could possibly want with a . . .'

'I want my assets and stock holdings protected,' Tammy chided mildly. 'If the marriage was to fall apart, and statistically that's quite possible considering that we're not in love, I don't want to have to share them.'

'You damn fool,' Jace barked. 'I'd sooner annul the marriage myself if it'll prove to you that I have no interests in your mediocre assets.'

'They may be mediocre to you,' Tammy defended, 'but they're everything to me.'

'If anyone needs protecting,' Jace rationalised, 'it's me against you. I have five times more value in stock, assets and holdings, not to mention my private investments. Enough to credit yours pitiful.'

'More reason for the pre-nuptial contract,' Tammy said easily. 'I'd like a clause stipulating that should the marriage dissolve, and it'll probably happen on the grounds that you'll fail to understand the concept of fidelity, then you'd have to compensate me financially, to an agreed amount of course.'

'You cheeky little devil,' Jace blazed, raising himself up from the table. 'Pre-nuptial agreements have no place in English law so if you think for one minute that I'm going to give you . . .' He paused.

Tammy felt her smile disintegrate as Jace's features revealed that he had tapped into her futile chain of thoughts. 'Nice try Tammy.' He folded his arms against his chest. 'Whatever you do, it's not going to change my mind about this marriage. Giving you my hard earned money certainly isn't. Only Hattie's recovery will put the brakes on.' He leaned curiously against the table. 'How much were you thinking on demanding?'

When she stayed mute, Jace lurched forward and grabbed her wrist impatiently. 'How much?'

'Three million,' Tammy blurted, twisting her wrist to free herself from his painful grip.

Jace's face hardened and his eyes glazed over cold. Without a word, he pulled a pen and notepad from his jacket pocket and jotted something down on a blank page. 'This is the partner acting and the name of the firm of my attorney.' He closed the pad before handing her the page he'd ripped out. 'Get your damn agreement drawn up and have my attorney approve it. If you think your grandmother's health warrants you a financial stake for your personal sacrifice in helping keep her alive, then I'll sign anything you want.'

Tammy's stomach turned sickly. So much for her ground rules. It had all backfired badly, as did everything she'd tried lately and as usual, she felt compelled to make amends.

In a low voice devoid of expression she said, 'Jace. I didn't mean that.' He was putting on his jacket. 'I just wanted you to see that I resent things being planned around me like I'm some kind of object about to be staged.' He began to put on his shoes. Tammy grew alarmed. 'Are you listening?' He had his back to her, walking toward the hallway. She followed him there. 'Jace!' He'd wrenched open the front door. 'I'm sorry.' Her last words were eclipsed with the door slam. Jace had left without a word, without even looking at her.

Tammy leaned against the doorframe. Something seemed to die inside her. She felt cold, empty and blessedly numb, for the pain was like an inflicted wound that doesn't bleed for several moments proceeding a deep, clean cut. Most of all, she felt achingly alone.

She walked slowly back into the sitting room, feeling a cold little knot form in the pit of her stomach as her eyes spotted the slim piece of black cloth lying discarded on the carpet. Jace had left in such a haste, he'd dropped his tie.

Tammy stooped to the floor and picked it up, holding it against her chest like her life depended on it. Her mind replayed the look on Jace's face as he'd left. She hadn't seen him so angry; she hadn't seen anyone so angry. His whole face had hardened like ice. She wondered if he'd ever be civilised to her again, let alone speak to her. It was a thought that troubled her immensely.

The doorbell suddenly peeled into her troubled mind, disrupting her chain of mingled thoughts. Tammy tensed. Jace had probably returned for his tie, or more precisely, to demand an apology from her. She certainly felt she owed him one, but he'd left in such a hurry, she knew he couldn't possibly have heard her. She was determined that he would now hear her out.

With hope in her heart, Tammy quickly made her way into the hallway and yanked open the front door. She stared in profound annoyance as Calvin stormed in and swept the hallway with a predatory glare.

'Where is he?' his agitated voice demanded as he marched into the sitting room. Unapposed, he carried on into the bedrooms preparatory to finding the culprit himself. Tammy slammed the door and went after him.

Calvin entered the kitchen. 'Is he here?'

She deliberately feigned ignorance. 'Who?'

Calvin's eyes narrowed sardonic. 'Taken to wearing a tie sis?'

Tammy transferred her gaze to her left hand and saw the tell-tale sign hanging there. 'Jace left five minutes ago,' she confirmed tight lipped. 'He stayed . . .'

'I know he stayed the night,' Calvin interrupted disgustedly. 'Sleeping with the enemy are we?'

'Now hold on one darn minute,' Tammy chided in a deadly tone. 'Don't you dare come in here flying off as though your standards are higher than mine. I didn't sleep with Jace.'

'Oh please,' Calvin scolded, his eyes bleak above the scornful twist of his mouth. 'You're expecting me to believe that a man like Jace Washington didn't take liberties with you last night? Come on sis, pigs fly.'

'The only person who took liberties with anyone last night was you,' Tammy hit back knowingly. 'I hope you knew it was Sherelle Tate under you and not somebody else like Martha Wilkes, your secretary.'

Calvin stepped back sheepishly. 'How did you know about . . .'

'You're tactless,' Tammy interrupted drily, 'on both counts. The whole office knows about you and Martha and it didn't take long for Jace to figure out who was sharing your bed this morning.'

Calvin blinked, his only sign of shameful emotion. It was a short-lived one. 'What was Jace doing answering your telephone anyway?'

'That's none of your business,' Tammy remarked airily. 'Why were you ringing?'

'I wondered how you were after last night,' Calvin conceded.

'I see,' Tammy tapped her feet in perverse annoyance. 'You mean after you announced to Jace and probably everyone there that I was a virgin?'

Calvin nervously headed for the wine cabinet and retrieved a bottle of brandy. 'I didn't mean that to happen,' he admitted, twisting the cap off the bottle. 'I was better for the champagne.'

'You could've come after me.'

'I would've, but, well . . .'

'Sherelle Tate caught your eye,' Tammy answered flatly. 'I can't say I'm surprised to whom you're duty-bound.'

'She told me this morning to ask you to forgive her, whatever that means,' Calvin explained lamely. He reached for a glass and poured in a large measure of brandy. 'I'm sorry too sis, but the last place I ever expected you to end up was in Jace Washington's arms.'

'Your lack of memory is becoming a constant worry to me,' Tammy said sarcastically. 'Who was it who said that I should think about all that's at stake? It would only be a small sacrifice if I married Jace Washington. Ring any bells?'

'I . . .'

'And only last night, who told me that it was time I got married and made *you* an uncle?'

'But . . .'

'Shut up Calvin,' Tammy snarled. 'Over these past few days, I've noticed that you've thought about nobody else but yourself. You haven't yet been to see grandma and you've left me out on a limb with Jace.' She marched toward him. 'Well I'm in this up to my eyeballs and you're in it with me. I need you and you're gonna need that drink. So sit down, shut up and listen to me.'

CHAPTER SEVEN

CALVIN'S FACE had turned a peculiar shade of burnished brown by the time Tammy concluded her speech - something she should have done a long time ago.

Their business relationship with their grandmother had deteriorated to the point where Hattie no longer considered them as prime candidates to continue the family heritage. She blamed Calvin for that and told him so. She held him responsible for Jace's interest in the company and more importantly, for his interest in her and blamed him for that too. Their grandmother's health was next on her agenda, as was the business of the wedding which was moving at a pace she'd never dreamt possible. She ended with the topic of Calvin's short-sightedness; that he hadn't seen Sherelle's ploy in using him as a weapon to make Jace jealous, even though Sherelle's attraction for Jace was one-sided.

Calvin had sat impatiently listening to all that she had to say, slowly sipping brandy with his expression unusually blank, but he pointedly refused to believe or be told that he'd been made a fool of by a woman. 'That's a lie,' he boomed, wide-eyed and one arm akimbo. 'I hope you have a damn good explanation for that remark.'

'I have my suspicions,' Tammy retaliated.

'Then keep them to yourself,' Calvin blazed in a low, threatening tone. 'I'll not have you bad talk Sherelle. I consider her to be one helluva lady.'

'Lady?' Tammy boomed. 'I think you're giving her more credit than she deserves.'

'I don't know what happened between you two,' Calvin

97

fumed, 'but she said she was sorry. I told you . . .'

'I know what you said,' Tammy interrupted. 'I just don't know whether to believe she'd have the grace to apologise. Like you, she suggested that I should get a pay off from Jace.'

'She suggested right,' Calvin answered with unswerving support. 'I still think you're making a mistake about not keeping the ring.'

'You're both unbelievable,' Tammy raged. 'Did it ever occur to you that I may just end up owning it, along with the title Mrs Jace P Washington?'

'I told you I'd take care of that,' Calvin bellowed so intensely, his glasses propped to the edge of his nose. 'You want it in writing?'

'Don't bother,' Tammy relented with as much venom, recalling that she'd learned to her own pain and anguish the consequences of a scheme backfired. 'You've already slept with plan A.'

'That does it,' Calvin rose abruptly from his seat and placed his empty brandy glass on the wine cabinet. 'I refuse to sit here and take any more of this shit,' he exclaimed tight-lipped. 'I have a plan B in reserve, but you're obviously not interested in hearing it.' He marched arrogantly toward the door. 'I also have to worry about the emergency board meeting scheduled for Monday and whether I can rely on some of the members who owe me a favour, but you don't want to hear about that either, so I'm leaving.'

'Wait a minute,' Tammy ran to the front door, shouting in dismay as Calvin made his way down the corridor that led to the main flight of stairs. 'What do you mean you have a plan B in reserve?' Calvin waved a dismissing hand in response and continued making his exit.

Tammy expelled a murderous squeal and intended chasing after him, but then realised she hadn't on any shoes. Storming back into her apartment, she slammed the door and cursed an oath beneath her breath.

Never again her mind reeled, spinning with chaotic thoughts. First an argument with Jace and then with Calvin. That had to be one of the worse mornings in her life.

She knew her brother meant well and that he'd always felt, after the death of their parents, that she was his responsibility to protect in life, but his tactics were wrong. She also knew that Jace's intentions were honourable and that he saw their engagement as a way of coaxing her grandmother back to health, but his strategy was agreeable only to him. She wanted nothing more than to curl up in a corner somewhere elusive, but her mind told her that it was time she went to see her grandmother.

Leaning against the door frame, Tammy swallowed a gulp of fresh air. Hattie would probably want to know how last night had turned out at the charity function and whether she'd made any further plans toward the wedding. She would have to omit all the controversial details of course, and adopt a bravado that would conceal the fact that Jace was probably not on speaking terms with her again.

There seemed no end to the level of performance she had to maintain. Maybe she should just give in and accept the possibility of marriage to Jace then she wouldn't have to pretend anymore. It would be easy. It seemed so easy, she told herself yearningly. The thought also scared Tammy to death.

IT WAS well after 2.00 pm when Tammy arrived at the hospital. Bracing herself outside her grandmother's room, she tossled her hair to give a confident outward projection and unbuttoned her black leather jacket to appear casual. She hadn't bothered to change her clothes, deciding instead to go as she had dressed earlier.

She wished Calvin had come along with her for she felt very much compelled to discuss the board meeting with their grandmother and the matter on which he'd unknowingly raised; which way was Hattie intending to vote?

With that thought uttermost on her mind, Tammy tapped a little knock on the door and ventured into the private ward. Four pair of eyes immediately rendered her paralysed.

Jace, dressed formally in a pale grey suit and patterned silk tie was seated at the foot of Hattie's bed and opposite him were seated two people in their mid sixties whom she presumed to be his parents.

Tammy was in shock. She hadn't known that Jace was planning on bringing his parents directly to see Hattie. Had she even suspected that they'd be visiting, she would've timed her arrival differently. She wasn't appropriately dressed to be introduced to her prospective in-laws and if first impressions were anything to go by, she couldn't possibly appear the picture of an executive's wife either.

She retreated a step backward. If her pulse quickened with apprehension, she told herself nervously, it was only because Jace's face was filled with impassive indifference at her arrival.

'Maybe I should come back later,' she stammered embarrassed, already pivoting on her heels to leave.

'But Tammy,' Hattie fussed, her voice confused. 'Me sure Jace's parents would like to meet you.'

'Come and sit next to me darling,' Jace immediately invited, his expression neutral.

Tammy obediently walked slowly toward the bed and smiled slightly as she reached Jace's parents. They nodded, a curt friendly inclination of their heads.

Mr Washington senior was a ranchy man, well stocked, broad shoulders and had the most arresting brandy coloured eyes Tammy had ever seen. He stood up as she passed by and held out a welcoming hand. 'Hello,' he spoked, unlike Jace, with a mild mannered Portugese accent. 'This is Jovita my wife and I am Jace senior.'

'Nice to meet you,' Tammy smiled in response, observing the remarkable resemblance of Jace that she saw in his mother, a slim petite woman whose carefully coiffed dark hair was her asset.

'And you must be the beautiful Tammy Caswell my son talk so fondly about on way here,' his father continued, retaking his seat.

Tammy flicked a surprised glance down at Jace whose cool, unscrutable eyes regarded her with a frank, rueful expression. 'I hope Jace didn't exaggerate,' she laughed nervously.

'Oh no,' Jovita returned warmly. 'He has under-estimated you. You are first girl he speak to us about.'

'Really,' Tammy answered with an odd note of sarcasm as she started to sit next to Jace, but as she did so, he caught her wrist and pulled her onto his lap. Her senses immediately jumped at the unexpected delight.

Jace's father laughed heartily. 'Ever so in love too,' he smiled.

'We wonder why he not talk of you earlier,' Jovita said hesitantly. 'Especially that you are my good friend Hattie's grandaughter. How long you see each other?'

Tammy opened her mouth and was about to speak when Jace's arms warily tightened around her waist. The essentially cautious gesture was unbearably sensuous to Tammy as Jace pressed his warm freshly shaven cheeks lightly against hers. 'It feels like forever, doesn't it darling?' he remarked.

'Er yes, it does,' Tammy said weakly, now alert to Jace's warning squeeze.

'They've been keeping it a secret for my sake,' Hattie intersected from her propped up pillow. 'Me suppose the way me ill and Jace's interest in fe me company has made things a little difficult for them.'

'Yes, I suppose it has,' Jovita sympathised. She rose from her chair and pressed a cream and gold handbag beneath her arm before retrieving a cardigan from the chair's back. 'Hattie, you would like to spend some time alone with your grandaughter, yes?' she intoned politely. 'So we will go now.'

'Eh eh,' Hattie chortled surprised. 'You a leave already when me want you to stay?'

'We are jetlag from the flight,' Jace's father interesected kindly. 'Jace and Tammy will tell us of their wedding plans tomorrow and we will call on you again before we go.'

Tammy cautiously directed her attention to Jace. 'Can I have a word with you alone, outside?' she whispered to him quietly, fighting the coil of tension that threatened to stifle her.

Jace gently released her, but deliberately kept one arm closed around her waist as they rose up from the bed and made toward the door.

'I'll be back in a minute,' Tammy told her grandmother before disappearing with Jace and his parents into the corridor.

Jace beckoned to his parents that he'd meet them at the elevator then took Tammy to one side out of their earshot. 'What is it?' he asked, his voice concerned.

'What would you expect?' Tammy grimaced quietly. 'Your parents actually *believe* that we're getting married.'

'So?' Jace shrugged.

'So, we're going to have to tell them the truth,' Tammy protested.

'We're doing nothing of the kind,' Jace responded coolly. 'Besides,' he added, 'you haven't anything to complain about. You're seeking a handsome financial reward for your efforts.'

Tammy flinched, seizing her opportunity to explain. 'That's not quite true,' she said ashamed. 'If we were forced to marry, my marriage vows would mean everything to me.'

'Especially at a gain of ten thousand a word.' Jace mocked.

'I can see there's no point in apologising to you,' Tammy sighed outwardly. 'I was beginning to think that my grandmother's rapid recovery was worth all the hassle and confrontation between us, but now, I'm not so sure. Now, I don't know whether to continue scheming against you or just leave you to carry on this farce by yourself.'

'You could do the easiest thing and give in,' Jace suggested.

'I could,' Tammy rationalised, looking over Jace's head at his parents who were waiting impatiently, 'but I would never be able to forgive myself for marrying a man who didn't love me.'

There was a deathly silence. Jace simply stood looking at her, his brown eyes subdued and enigmatic. When he finally spoke, his expression was warred with bewilderment. 'Kiss me,' he coaxed softly.

Tammy closed her eyes, agonisingly aware of the deep stir in her body. 'No,' she told him vehemently.

'My parents are watching,' Jace said by way of persuasion.

'I don't care,' Tammy admonished, almost absently.

'I care,' Jace insisted, drawing her bodily into his arms. His voice suddenly deepened seductively. 'I care very much.'

The moment his lips touched hers, Tammy instinctively knew that Jace's remark hinted on an innuendo that he might actually care for her. She wasn't sure what to make of it. On the one hand, he'd offered himself, he'd offered marriage and now, it seemed, he was offering his affections, however limited. But could she, on the other hand, accept that in preference to love?

Certainly, the way in which he was kissing her made her alarmingly aware that she could just about accept anything. His slow seduction stripped away her defences so subtly, she was hardly conscious of it.

Jace didn't overpower her. There was something different in his kiss this time. His tongue gently outlined the shape of her lips, probing delicately with a sensual suggestion.

Deaf to everthing but the dictates of her own body, Tammy sighed softly and willingly put her arms around his neck. With a growl of satisfaction, Jace's arms closed around her, drawing her into an embrace that re-acquainted Tammy with every hard muscle in his lean, male body. His kiss deepened into a promise of delight as his hands sought the small of her back to caress the smoothness of her skin above the waistline of her jeans.

Tammy returned his kiss with an abandon completely foreign to her until now, lost in the fantasy of a man she seemed destined to meet all her life. She was floating in a time so detached from real time, where nothing existed except the prince of her fantasy, that she felt totally bereft when Jace finally released her.

'I don't believe I did that,' she said shakily, leaning against the wall behind her to steady her balance.

'There's a lot you still have to learn about yourself,' Jace clarified shakily. 'You can start with admitting to your sexual desires and,' he traced an unsteady finger down her cheek, 'be a bit more forgiving with yourself.' With that comment, he dug his hands into his pockets and walked over to the elevator.

Tammy stared after him, swept away by Jace's power of persuasion, overawed with the feeling that she'd been successfully analysed, and knowing that she was most definitely in love.

Turning on her heels, she re-entered her grandmother's room, wishing she knew more about Jace, his inner thoughts and his inner feelings. But Jace was like an unsolved case. Even the initial P of his middle name was a mystery to her.

'You like Jace's parents?' Hattie asked softly as she watched Tammy cut short the distance between them.

'Yes, they're nice,' Tammy answered, forcing her attention to one of the chairs opposite the bed. 'How are you today grandma?'

'The consultant come round this morning,' Hattie said with a pinch of optimism. 'They say me will probably be discharged in a couple of days, but what do they know?'

'They happen to know a great deal,' Tammy spoke with delight. 'That means you're getting better.'

'Am I? And better for what?' Hattie looked bewildered. 'Sometimes me no know anymore.'

'You still have the business,' Tammy smiled, 'and us. We wouldn't be here without you.'

'Calvin no come see me yet,' Hattie said sadly.

'Well - Calvin's . . .' Tammy couldn't find the words to defend or explain away Calvin's behaviour.

'There's nothing you can say,' Hattie reasoned weakly. 'That's why me so glad you a marry Jace. Me know his mama for forty two years and me know Jace build himself up from nothing. Me so proud of that godson. Calvin have every opportunity, every chance to make something of himself. You must know me very disappointed?'

'I suspected,' Tammy nodded.

'Well you right,' Hattie propped herself up on her elbow, her face painfully set and hard. 'Me a vote by proxy on Monday and me give fe me vote already to Randall Garvey. Me just want you to know that me a do the right thing for everybody.'

Tammy's eyes zoomed in on her grandmother. 'Does that mean . . .'

'It means that the Board accept my resignation,' Hattie interrupted, 'and them a go elect a new chief executive. Me going to spend what left of my retirement in hope of seeing my great-grandchildren, which reminds me. What you a do 'bout the wedding?'

When Tammy finally left her grandmother an half hour later, her mind was running overtime with the orders and counter-orders Hattie had passed to her verbally and listed on the piece of paper in her hand.

She felt suddenly nauseated that her life was being

carried into a situation that simply wasn't going to happen. Her grandmother's recovery meant that she would be discharged in a day or two and that in turn meant no wedding. Hattie would be strong enough to take the disappointment and she could return Jace his ring.

The ring. Tammy's eyes sliced over to the diamond rock that sparkled eloquently on her finger. Looking at it, she felt very much engaged. She also felt newly charged and excited over the prospect of getting married and having children. The thought that it was all a pretense pushed forward in her mind, but she shoved it aside. For now, she wanted to believe that it was real, believe that Jace was in love with her and that they were going to live happily ever after.

She spent the rest of the day churning over that very thought. It fogged her mind as she ate dinner alone and lingered endlessly whilst she watched TV. Finally, she retired to her bedroom and undressed before turning out the lights and pulling over the bed covers. As she lay there in the dark, Tammy made the biggest decision of her life. She would give in to Jace's assimilation of their romance and play her role to the fullest. She would also forgive herself the consequences, if only for the sake of love.

TAMMY AWOKE the following morning to the shrill of the telephone. Turning on her side, she picked up the receiver and heard Jace's soft voice alert her attention.

'Tammy, are you awake?' he queried unsure.

'What time is it?' Tammy mumbled in response, blinking her eyelids.

'6.00 am.'

'What?'

'I called to tell you about dinner.'

'Dinner?'

'It'll be at my place and I'll call for you sometime around 3 O'clock.'

'Couldn't you have phoned later to tell me that?'

Tammy answered, though she was glad to hear his voice.

'No,' Jace answered somberly.

'Why not?'

'Because I couldn't sleep last night for thinking about you,' Jace mocked. 'You've got me totally bewitched.'

Tammy's mouth curtailed into a wry smile. 'Have I?' she said, trying unsuccessfully to hide the joy in her voice. 'How sad.'

'Isn't it.' Jace jabbed.

'What do you intend to do about it?' she asked, savouring the crazy warmth that seeped through her body.

'Nothing,' Jace's voice was glacial and firm. 'Your grandmother is getting well so it's just a matter of time before the situation is made easy for you to leave.' He was on the point of hanging up.

'Wait!' The exclamation was forced out of her as Tammy rejected the sudden acute shock which Jace's remark had on her. 'Why are you telling me this?'

There was a short silence. Tammy held her breath until Jace said drily, 'Damned if I know.' He hung up.

Tammy replaced the receiver and turned onto her back, suddenly feeling frightened, disillusioned and utterly confused.

THE TIME was almost 3 O'clock when Tammy heard the knock at the front door indicating that Jace had arrived to collect her.

She'd ventured from her bed at sometime around noon and had prepared herself toast and coffee before seating herself at the kitchen table to reflect on the conversation she'd had with Jace earlier that morning. The echo of his words, even now, served as a harsh reminder of their true relationship.

In a way, she felt like something that had been used and then discarded because it was no longer useful. They had begun to know each other and somehow she felt so close to him - surely he felt close to her too. Jace couldn't possibly intend to just forget about her.   But he could, her mind warned. She'd read enough about his affairs to know that.

Deciding on putting him completely out of her mind, she'd flicked open the pages of the *Sunday Times*, and was instantly propelled into yet another topic of her life as she spotted, almost immediately, the article that made reference to her grandmother's company. It read:-

'CASWELL COSMETIC'S LATEST EFFORTS TO SECURE A REPLACEMENT FOR MAMA HATTIE CASWELL, ITS FORMER CHAIRPERSON AND CHIEF EXECUTIVE WHO HAS RECENTLY RESIGNED DUE TO ILL HEALTH, WILL COME TO AN END ON MAY 25, ALMOST A WEEK AFTER HER DEPARTURE.

'THE HEADHUNTERS ORIGINAL LIST OF CANDIDATES THOUGHT TO BE CONSIDERED FOR THE JOB HAVE ALL BEEN DISMISSED AS UNSUITABLE AND SPECULATORS BELIEVE THIS TO INCLUDE MAMA HATTIE'S ONLY GRANDSON.

'AN INSIDER COMMENTED THAT THE BOARD OF DIRECTORS, MEETING TOMORROW, ARE SEEKING A HIGH-PROFILE CANDIDATE WHO POSSESSES THAT UNIQUE BRAND OF DEVELOPMENT AND FINANCIAL EXPERTISE THAT THEY REQUIRE.

'THERE IS SOME SPECULATION THAT JACE PETHUEL WASHINGTON JR, WHO OWNS A STRING OF COMPANIES UNDER WASHINGTON INTERNATIONAL LIMITADA AND WHO IS ALSO ENGAGED TO YOUNG MISS CASWELL, MAY SCOTCH HIS PLANS TO BUY OUT THE COMPANY IF ELECTED FOR THE POST.

'WASHINGTON, AN AFRO-BRAZILIAN AGED 34, IS TIPPED AS THE HOT FAVOURITE AFTER HIS BLOCK PURCHASES OF CASWELL STOCK. CITY ANALYSTS BELIEVE THAT, IF APPOINTED, HE WILL . . .' She closed the newspaper.

Her first reaction had been relief over the knowledge that she'd finally discovered what Jace's middle initial stood for. Her second, a measure of sympathy for Calvin who was an avid digester of the Sunday press and would, most certainly, have seen that particular article.

Whilst in her bedroom, deciding on what to wear, uncertain about how to change her image to appear more formal, her third reaction was to try and again persuade Jace not to accept the post if it were offered him.

After selecting and rejecting numerous outfits, she'd finally settled on a cream suit with a printed silk blouse; the background of which was a vivid grey, the colour of her mood.

Jace wouldn't dream of turning down the post for Calvin, she'd decided later, carefully braiding her black hair at the back. It was enough that he'd suggested that her brother would bribe some of the members. It was also aggravating having to hear those things being said about Calvin, more so because not only were they true, but she also had to play an ingenue's role with the glamorous man who directed them - the man she loved and who was now waiting for her outside her apartment.

Tammy felt a combination of excitement and apprehension as she crossed her sitting room into the hallway and opened the front door. Jace was lounging with one hand braced high against the doorframe, dressed in stone washed jeans and a pale blue coloured cotton shirt under a tweedy jacket that emphasized the width of his powerful shoulders.

Her expression of mortified horror at his casual apparel brought a grin to his face. 'Don't worry,' he commented wryly, comprehending her alarm. 'Mum won't mind if you're a little formal. Are you ready?'

'Yes,' Tammy nodded, closing the door behind her and following Jace over to his BMW parked out on the road.

It was the first time she'd ever seen him in clothes other than a suit and she was forced to admit how strikingly handsome and informal his outward attire collaborated the more boyish and blossoming personality that was reflected. It was a side of him that Tammy yearned to know, but which she felt sure was rarely seen. Taking the passenger seat beside him, she watched as Jace ignited the engine and surged the car forward.

'I suppose you know what the press are saying?' she said casually enough to appear disinterested.

'I did have occasion to read *The Voice* yesterday,' Jace answered calmly, his eyes fixed on the road.

Tammy hesitated, unsure on how she was going to proceed. 'Are you going to take the job if it's offered to you tomorrow?'

'I don't think you want to hear the answer to that,' Jace countered disquietly.

'Well if you do,' Tammy pressed nonetheless, 'I can't imagine for one minute that Calvin or even Jason Lee would entertain the thought of working under you.'

'That's a matter of opinion,' Jace remarked lightly, but not lightly enough. Tammy detected a movement in his jaw as he continued. 'I'm sure Jason Lee's committed loyalty to the company will hold as long as he still fancies his chances with you.'

Tammy suddenly felt uncomfortable in her seat. 'Jason and I are just friends and that's all,' she affirmed quickly, startled that Jace should even mention of any communion between them. 'I've worked with him a few times and . . .'

'Turned down his passes,' Jace interrupted.

Tammy averted her gaze nervously, disliking the direction of the conversation. She couldn't fathom why as she had nothing to hide, except maybe the onetime kiss she'd given Jason two years ago at Calvin's pre-Christmas party and the fact that she'd told Jason how she felt about Jace which, although untrue at the time, was pretty much true now. Her only worry was whether that trust had left Jason's lips to travel the corporate grapevine.

If it had, Jace had probably heard something and was

now deliberating that particular topic to get the admission out of her. His cryptic phone call of that morning was enough to raise her suspicions.

She decided to play it safe and remain urbane and detached. 'Jason's quite harmless,' she said evenly.

'Nobody's harmless,' Jace debated in response. 'Not if they're normal.'

'Well you're normal enough,' Tammy mouthed smoothly. 'You've been a constant threat to everyone's peace of mind since your arrival in London. How far do you intend to go before we can all feel safe again?'

'Now there's a tempting question,' Jace mocked.

'Seriously?'

'I'm not unserious.'

'Well?'

'I take it you're referring to the possibility that if I don't become CEO tomorrow, then I may still decide to buy-out the company and dismantle some of its assets to sell off?'

Tammy nodded. 'I have to know one way or the other. What are you planning to do?'

Jace glanced sideways irritably. 'Whatever I'm planning, it will be for the common good of the company,' he said firmly.

Tammy leaned back against her seat, knowing from Jace's tone that he was not going to prolong that particular discussion. She felt as though she'd gone right back to square one, none the wiser as to what card Jace intended to play than her brief knowledge of him when they'd first met.

All her endeavours, her scheming and Calvin's lame attempts to be rid of him had gone ludicrously wrong. Jace had skilfully eluded their shoddy work of art with the dexterity of a maestro and was still able to go ahead with his plans as scheduled. Plans that could mean a very different life for her and Calvin.

The car pulled up outside a building well secluded by trees and overlooking Regent's Park. Jace left the car first and directed her inside the building to the top floor where he lived in a rooftop penthouse that enjoyed enviable views of the park.

Jovita was at the door to meet them, an apron around her slim waist protecting the peach crepe-de-chine dress she wore beneath. 'Hello Tammy,' she said warmly. 'Come in. I cook especially for you today.'

Tammy smiled curtly as her feet sunk into the plush beige carpet that led from the hallway into a well decorated lounge. Jace's father was sat comfortably among a flight of cream leather sofas, his eyes heavily trained on the TV set, totally absorbed in a soccer match. He was so engrossed, he failed to see her arrive until she'd taken the seat opposite him. Even so, his only reponse was a slight inclination of his head.

'You will ignore my husband,' Jovita waved a dismissing hand in annoyance. 'Nothing comes between him and a soccer match.'

Tammy chuckled. 'It's okay, really.'

'I go into the kitchen and finish up dinner,' Jovita added softly. 'Please, make yourself comfortable.'

The thought of being left with Jace immediately sent spasms of nerves down Tammy's spine. It wasn't because she didn't want to be close to him, she did, but enduring another topical conversation on their impending marriage or the company wasn't the kind of stimulation she'd planned.

By way of seeking some solitude to think, she turned to Jovita and offered, 'Would you like me to help you in the kitchen?'

'Oh no,' Jovita said startled. 'You are our guest. Jace will take care of you.'

As Jovita left, Jace stood over Tammy, his eyes politely attentive as he asked softly, 'Would you like something to drink?'

Tammy answered shyly, her eyes downcast. 'I'll have a glass of mineral water with lemon and ice please.'

She couldn't quite account for the sudden tremor inside her, whether it was the vastness of the room or the imposing gaze which Jace directed her way. Secretly, Tammy knew it to be the latter, for in that brief second before Jace went to fetch her drink, his brown eyes had flared with warmth and a . . . proudness that he was honoured she'd come there.

Seconds later, he returned, handing her the tall, clear glass. 'Chilled mineral water with lemon,' he clarified, taking the seat next to her.

Tammy took the glass firmly. 'Thank you.'

Jace ripped open his can of beer then said, 'I went to see Hattie this morning.'

Tammy's eyes widened instantly. 'And?'

'Apparently, her consultant confirmed that she will definitely be discharged on Tuesday,' Jace said smoothly. 'Unfortunately, I won't be here so you'll have to make the necessary arrangements to take her home.'

'That's great news,' Tammy smiled brightly. 'You've no idea how relieved I am.'

'About your grandmother or to be rid of me?' Jace countered quietly.

Tammy's eyes immediately shot to his forlorn expression. Jace suddenly seemed so innocent, vulnerable and totally bereft, she didn't quite know how to react.

They both knew that Hattie's discharge would ultimately mean an end to the pretense and assimilation of their romance. To her chagrin, Tammy felt a degree of unhappiness about that and yet she was so elated over her grandmother's remarkable recovery too. It was a disturbing duo of emotions that caused her to gabble. 'I - I was implying about my grandmother,' she stammered quickly.

She wanted to tell Jace there and then that she loved him, that she would be his forever, but somehow the words failed to emerge. Jace didn't love her in return and like he'd said that morning, he planned to go no further with their escapade.

In two days, she would be on her own again. Jace would no longer be her significant other and she would no longer have any claim to him. It was a thought Tammy couldn't bear to think about.

CHAPTER EIGHT

TAMMY CONSIDERED ignoring the doorbell when it rang at 8.30 am the following morning, even though she realised the futility of such an act.

Whoever it was, wasn't going to give up merely because she failed to answer the door. The constant ringing indicated that it was someone who obviously wanted to talk to her and that meant either Jace or Calvin. Secretly, Tammy wished it was neither.

Her dinner engagement with Jace and his parents the night before had created more havoc that she could cope with. Firstly, there was the discovery that Jace had an adopted sister, his younger sister having died from whopping cough as a baby. His mother had since decided to foster neglected children and, despite their own impoverished lifestyle, Marchi was adopted when Jace was fourteen. She was now a graduate professor in psychology and had already planned to cut short her scheduled holiday in Trinidad to be at their wedding.

There was then talk that she and Jace should build a second home in Brazil, she selling her flat in London and Jace letting out the penthouse when they were not staying there. Despite the delicious vegetable soup, which was about the only thing she felt able to eat, and amid the discussions and family talk over a traditional Brazilian dinner, she'd felt isolated, stifled and totally betrayed.

Jace hadn't once suggested to her that his family were already making plans for a wedding they believed was to take place in just under two months. That alarmed her immensely, for she wondered what possible explanation

they would give when the time came to call off their
engagement.

It was obvious from Jace's reserved expression that he
hadn't given that much thought at all. Infact, as the night
drew on and they later ate dessert and talked, by tacit
consent, on light and general topics of interest, she noticed
that he'd adopted a far away look in his eyes, launching
into a world of his own and only momentarily descending
from it when he'd briefly defended his outrageous
behaviour at an uncle's house, aged nine.

Jovita had begun to reminiscene about the past, telling
her of the many mischievous tricks Jace would play as a
boy. She learned that he was an adorable child, doted upon
by all who'd met him. *'The most charming, stubborn dark
haired imp you'd even seen,'* Jovita had intoned. She'd
listened avidly to all that was said, helplessly eager to learn
everything about the powerful, dynamic man who owned
her heart, but didn't seem to want it.

Once their eyes had locked and a fierce spasm shot
through her entire nervous system like lightening. It only
served as a reminder of how badly she wanted Jace.

When the night finally ended, she was abundantly
relieved to go home. Jace's father had returned to the
lounge for late night soccer via satellite and Jovita had
retired to her bed for the night.

The ride back to Kensington was, as she'd expected, a
silent one, but when the BMW finally pulled up outside her
apartment and she'd made to get out of the car, Jace
pulled her back into her seat.

'We're going to have to come to a decision,' he told her
tautly.

'A decision about what?' she asked. For a fleeting
moment, she was hopeful. Hopeful that he was going to say
that they should get married after all and treat the whole
facade as reality, but she was to be disappointed.

'We're going to have to decide on a story that would
explain, without too much comment, our break-up, and

preferably,' Jace added with caution, 'something that won't alarm your grandmother a great deal.'

Tammy didn't know what to say. What could she say? Jace had advocated from the outset that once her grandmother was well, the deal would be off, so to speak and he was keeping his end of that promise. So who was she to argue?

'Aren't you afraid of the effects such a story would have in the financial sector and the media?' she queried, prolonging the inevitable task of plotting their severed ties.

'The shares will take a short fall, but nothing that cannot be rectified in time,' Jace reassured. 'I thought a simple agreement of incompatibility would suffice. Your grandmother could be spared the heartache and your reputation would remain intact.'

'My reputation is already widely speculated,' she reminded. 'You hinted at that once yourself. I don't know why you just don't agree to an affair situation and have done with it.'

'And risk your grandmother another relapse?' Jace breathed. 'Obviously you're not thinking.'

I didn't think I would be allowing the man I love to leave me, she'd told herself helpless. 'What do you have in mind?' she asked, biting her lips to dissipate the dizzying rush of apprehension.

'You could hint to your grandmother that you're not happy with things,' Jace hesitated. 'Tell her you're not in love with me.'

Tammy gasped. 'Isn't that a bit heavy?'

'It's true isn't it?' Jace jabbed. 'You shouldn't have any problems getting that one across.'

'No - no, I shouldn't,' she'd lied, not daring to look at him.

'So we're in agreement?'

Tammy nodded, afraid that her voice would betray her.

'Why the long face?' Jace suddenly queried sardonic. 'I thought you'd be congratulating yourself. You're going to get what you've always wanted, to be rid of me, though you'd be three million short of course.'

'You can keep your damn money,' Tammy spat. 'I never wanted it in the first place. I wanted . . .'

'What?' Jace challenged.

I want you to love me, Tammy thought. 'Nothing,' she said.

The tension was like an invisible wire between them that stretched to breaking point by the time she'd left the car and reached her apartment door. Jace had followed her up, his silence grating against her nerves like sandpaper.

For the first time in her life since the death of her parents, she'd felt totally alone and alienated. It was a horrible feeling, like something inside her had been cut away. She tried to tell herself how ridiculous that must be, that she couldn't possibly have harboured such feelings for a man in just a few days, but the emotions remained nonetheless and Tammy couldn't shake them however much she tried.

As she placed her key inside the lock, Jace said tightly, 'I won't ask if I should be counting on your vote tomorrow.'

'It'd be unethical of me to tell you anyway,' she said obstinately. It was the last thing she recalled saying to him as she closed the door.

Now, with a deep sigh, she levered her slender figure out of bed, slipping into her bedcoat as she contemplated facing the ordeal of answering the door.

Tammy was dimly aware that there was a great deal of anguish under her present lethargy, but she pushed the knowledge from her consciousness. Nothing could hurt her as long as she continued to exist in this vacuum, she thought on opening the front door.

'Tammy, I'm sorry to call on you so early in the morning,' Jason Lee apologised sheepishly. 'Can I come in, it's important?'

Startled, and somewhat relieved that she was not faced

with Jace or Calvin, Tammy gestured Jason to come inside her apartment then closed the door. 'What is it?' she inquired, inviting him to sit down as she joined him.

'Who are you voting for today?' Jason prodded grimly.

'Jason, you know that's privy information,' Tammy returned steadily. 'I can't just tell you that.'

'I'm afraid Calvin may not have enough votes to win over the election to chief executive,' Jason coaxed.

'How do you know that?' Tammy immediately queried. When Jason's face clouded, her eyebrows rose in comprehension. 'Calvin's bribed some of the members and you're an accessary after the fact.'

'This isn't a nursery game,' Jason gritted his teeth. 'If Jace Washington gets in, it'll be the end of Caswell Cosmetics as we know it.'

'I can't believe you two would stoop so low,' Tammy said embittered by their deceit, the hurt evident in her voice. 'If anyone ever finds out that you've financially bribed...'

'They won't,' Jason assured. 'We've seen to that.'

Tammy stared at him in annoyance. 'You've been a good ancillary to my grandmother Jason. Why on earth have you allowed Calvin to get you involved?'

'Isn't that obvious?' Jason sighed.

'What - what do you mean?' Tammy answered nervously.

'With Calvin at the helm, maybe you and I could...'

'Maybe you didn't pay any attention to what I told you the other day,' Tammy interrupted bluntly.

'Dammit Tammy, you've only known the man a few days,' Jason grimaced jealously. 'Hardly time to fall in love.'

'I know it all probably sounds like something out of a romantic fiction novel to you,' Tammy agreed. 'Assimilated relationships are a joke right? Well, I fell in love with him, but that doesn't matter now because the wedding is off.'

Jason's eyes immediately glittered in response. 'What happened?'

'What didn't happen?' Tammy laughed with an ache in her throat. 'The latest was my demand for a three million pre-nup.'

'What?' Jason nearly fell out of his seat. 'I thought you said you loved him.'

'The pre-nup was a mistake,' Tammy explained sadly. 'I wanted to hurt him. I think he'll be more than happy to be rid of me now.'

'Which is precisely what I can say of him,' Jason said without shame or sympathy. 'I just hope you know with whom your loyalty lies at the meeting today.'

'I resent that remark,' Tammy chided with a hint of venom. 'I know exactly who I'm going to vote for. Now if you'll excuse me, I'd like to get dressed.'

Jason rose awkwardly out of his chair and made toward the door. 'Remember,' he reminded before leaving. 'Calvin's your brother and he needs you now more than ever.'

As Tammy closed the Regency style door and made toward her bedroom, her mind lingered on Jason's last comment. Calvin didn't need her, she shrugged scornfully. If she could be bought for a price then maybe he'd need her. Since the death of their parents, the only thing Calvin had ever cared about was himself, money, leisure and women. She suddenly felt foolishly credulous that she hadn't realised that sooner.

For in his moment of dire strait, when he needed unswerving support from those he knew, his only recourse was the lowest form of deceit, bribery. That annoyed her immensely.

Flinging off her nightgown, she swung open the wardrobe doors. Calvin could never hold the job down a full year before he tired of boredom, she thought maliciously. He'd just grow more bawdy, more outrageous and definitely more party conscious. No, she sighed wearily. Calvin couldn't possibly do the job.

Jace Washington could though, her brain deducted logically. He was the epitome of strength, the engine that steered the wheels of industry, commerce and finance. Now he wanted to inject that same majestic force into afro cosmetics and become the company's main power source.

And he could do it too, she thought having recalled that she'd just recently read a report on him in *Black Enterprise* who'd ranked his company as the second largest Ethnic-owned and operated business in Brazil. Washington International Limitada had been bestowed the prestigious title of *'Company of the Year'* in honour of its innovation and progress in the corporate business sector, offering even stronger presence in America, the Caribbean and Africa, Europe being its new target market.

Her body straightened in awe and pride at the sudden realisation that her decision had to be what was right for the shareholders and the company at large. In truth, her emotions told her nothing more other than she had to vote for the man she loved.

THE MOMENT Tammy entered the boardroom, dressed in a deep crimson suit, her purple handbag pressed curtly beneath her arm, she felt precariously as though she had just been presented with a dilemma. Fourteen male faces immediately strayed their attention to the door where she stood, their expressions displaying perverse annoyance at her obvious untimely presence.

Because all the men in attendance were commercial giants whose time was extremely valuable, everyone was asked to be punctual. The meeting was to convene precisely at 9.30 am, but she had arrived at 9.45 am.

'I'm - I'm terribly sorry,' Tammy informed the thunderous-looking group, immediately seeking refuge in the nearest available chair at the table and vowing beneath her breath that it was past time she learned how to drive. 'I . . .'

'Let's get on with it,' a jowly man demanded unsympatetically.

Tammy nervously placed her bag on the table and caught Calvin's outraged glare of impotent hostilty. He had already surmised that her late arrival could cost him dearly as it would probably have some reflection on the vote for him.

Forcing her gaze westward to escape his ire, her eyes locked on Jace's steely cool gaze. He was at the opposite end of the table, immaculately attired and projecting an impressive outwardly image.

She detected a shallow depth of warmth in his eyes that twisted a tight cord of desire in her groin. Sucking in her breath, Tammy dragged her eyes away from him and steered them toward Randall Garvey who was calling the vote.

White slips of paper were circulated by the company secretary and everyone was ordered to clearly state the name of the person who they wished to replace her grandmother, Mama Hattie, to chief executive and chairman of the company.

The members were informed that Hattie's vote was being carried by proxy and that Jace had that morning become a member of the Board, news which earned a blatant look of derision from Calvin.

An atmosphere of supreme hush and supressed tension evaded the entire room as the company secretary collected the folded slips of paper and placed them all neatly in a pile directly within Randall's reach.

Tammy felt her hands tremor and risked looking at Calvin, her heart heavy with the knowledge of what she'd taken away from him. His facade had weakened to a nervous and bothered man, the perspiration evident across his flustered forehead. Jason Lee sipped water from a small glass in an attempt to prohibit any further tiny bubbles of sweat to shadow his face and five other members kept their heads downcast, almost in fear of being caught out in their bribery.

Tammy felt compelled to look at Jace and chart his reaction, but didn't want to distract herself from the inevitable outcome. Yet, as Randall began to count out the votes in a slow progression of name calling, she couldn't resist taking a peek at him. Jace's face was set firm and hard, his brown eyes fixed steadfast on Randall.

Tammy had to marvel at his stamina. After months of pre-meditated block share purchases and careful strategic planning, she expected to see some semblance of apprehension, panic even, etched into his granite profile. Instead, there was not so much as a flicker of betrayal in Jace's cool, stolid expression. At that precise moment, she wondered what he was thinking and whether she featured in his thoughts at all.

Then suddenly, as though some psychic phenomena was at work, his gaze glanced crossward and settled on her hazel, inquiring eyes. Tammy's whole body warmed with the unexpected delight of his attention. Why, she wondered stupidly, did her silly little heart turn over everytime he looked at her.

She thought ludicrously whether Jace had some telepathic knowledge that she'd voted for him. It was the only explanation that sprung to her dismantled mind to warrant the genuine smile of tenderness in his face. A smile that was enough to hold her captivated until the sudden gasp of raised anticipation echoed across the room and detached Jace's attention from her.

His eyes shifted immediately to Randall and her own focussed in on Calvin, aware that the vote had been unanimously decided. Calvin looked as vulnerable as a lost child and Jason's face seemed equally as upset, though she couldn't quite tell as he'd buried his head into the pit of his hands.

Suddenly, she felt oblivious to it all, even though her eyes caught sight of Randall slumping heavily into his chair in total relief that it was all over. There was only one explanation for the sudden occurrence of events. Jace Washington had become the new CEO and chairman of Caswell Cosmetics Plc.

Tammy turned to find that Jace had risen from his chair, the gleam of triumph sparkling in his brown eyes adding a charismatic flair of strength into his features which she found breathtakingly erotic.

'Members of the Board,' his chin lifted preparatory to making a speech. 'This is a momentuous occasion for . . .'

'Momentuous occasion for what?' Calvin's mad outburst rudely interrupted Jace midstream and raised a few worried eyebrows. 'You've stolen what is rightfully mine and I'm not going to let you get away with it. I'll be contesting your sovereignty to my kingdom you bastard.'

Tammy's eyes zoomed virulently on Calvin, her mind wishing she was anywhere at that precise moment in time except where she was presently.

'It seems your fawning and pandering to my grandmother's wishes has ascended you to the throne with the princess' hand in marriage,' Calvin continued regardless of the fourteen horrified glances.

'Calvin!' Tammy restrained embarrassed for him as well as herself. 'Don't, please.' Her voice failed to carry weight. She risked looking at Jace and caught the same fiery glare of contempt and black rage mirrored into every inch of his face. Alarm rippled along her limps as she thought wildly how to curtail the situation.

'Don't you dare Calvin me,' her brother returned scathingly, taking her completely aback. 'Your oscar winning performance deserves an academy award the way you've starred in your role as the devoted wife-to-be. I'd say you've more than earned the three million you asked for, though I'm surprised you finally took my advice about the pay-off. Be sure to keep the ring too. It's worth a mint.'

The tears prickled in Tammy's eyes as she side-glanced Jason Lee with a punishing look of hate. He hadn't wasted any time informing her brother about their conversation that morning. The best she could do now was to get Calvin out of the boardroom before he decided on disclosing any further information that would damage their reputation. 'Calvin, please . . .'

'Well Mr Washington,' Calvin waived her protest aside and redirected his attention toward Jace. 'What do you intend to do now? Sell off the company assets for a quick profit or pay my sister for services rendered?'

Calvin never got an answer. Before Tammy could even blink, Jace had strided the length of the table, his fists clenched hard as a rock and jabbed Calvin with a knuckled right upper cut which landed squarely on his jaw. The whole room fell into silence as Calvin slumped to the floor, spread eagled and out cold sober.

Humiliation roared through Tammy, screaming in her ears and bellowing in her head as thirteen pair of eyes turned to pity her with their commiseration for her brother's disorderly conduct.

Seizing her bag from the table, she rose out of her chair and ran hastily from the room. Jace was quick to follow and caught up with her outside the conference suite that preceded the boardroom.

'Tammy wait,' he shouted, catching hold of her wrist with enough force to restrain her.

Tammy turned to face him, her emotions well guarded as she succeeded in holding back the tears which threatened. 'What do you want Jace?'

'Your instincts to walk out were correct,' he said in a menacingly soft voice. 'It must be hard watching the wheels finally come off your brother's trolley.'

'Calvin isn't losing his mind,' Tammy snapped, her voice quivering.

A muscle moved convulsively in Jace's jaw. 'Now did I say that he was?'

Tammy dipped her head to avoid looking at him.

'It wasn't my fault what happened back there and well

you know it,' he explained. 'I came after you to apologise, but I'd have been a total idiot if I were to take that kind of abuse lying down. I'm just sorry you had to witness that ugly scene.'

'What are you going to do about him?' she queried with renewed concern.

Jace tightly clenched his jaw. 'Right now, I'm hovering over the notion of firing him.'

'Don't,' Tammy implored quickly. 'He's insecure at the moment. Calvin doesn't know what he's saying sometimes.'

'But you decided nonetheless to take his advice and now the whole company knows about your pre-nuptial demand,' Jace jabbed in response.

Tammy looked at him with pain-dazed eyes, fighting down the tears that again tugged at her weakness. 'I'm past explaining that,' she said inanely, lowering her head to the sparkling diamond on her left hand. Removing it from her finger, she handed it toward him. 'I believe this belongs to you.'

Alarm flickered in Jace's gaze as he allowed her to drop the ring into the palm of his hand.

'I wish I could say it was good while it lasted,' she said calmly, swallowing the lump of desolution in her throat, 'but it would just sound like a postcard sentiment.'

Jace's forehead creased into a dark frown of bemused irritation. 'You don't need to do this,' he said solemnly, looking disbelieving at the ring.

'Yes I do,' Tammy countered firmly. 'It's worth a mint isn't it? Besides, grandma's going to be discharged tomorrow and you've got what you wanted, chairmanship of Caswell.'

'Our agreement had nothing to do with me wanting to become chairman,' Jace chided confused. 'It was for Hattie's sake.'

'And she won't be in hospital come this time tomorrow,' Tammy reminded. 'That *was* our agreement wasn't it?'

Jace cast his eyes sideways with impatience. 'I know what I said Tammy,' he admitted, 'but you haven't explained anything to your grandmother. Don't you think it'd be better to wait until she was well on the way to recovery before you decide on making any rash decisions?'

Tammy hadn't thought of that. Her grandmother would no doubt question her immediately about the ring and she could be forced to explain the circumstances prematurely. 'I - I . . .'

'Wear the ring,' Jace insisted, instantly replacing the diamond on her left finger. 'At least until I get back from Brazil.'

'We'll seldom be seeing each other again when you return,' Tammy persisted. 'I've decided it'll be for the best if I resign my position here at the company and you'll be busy running it. I'm sure you wouldn't mind if I think up someting to tell . . .'

'I do mind,' Jace interrupted. 'There isn't a problem with you holding on to it. I'll be back in two weeks after I re-organise my business affairs in Brazil with my father. Maybe then, we can talk.'

'I can't imagine what we could possibly have to say to one another,' Tammy retorted. 'You've already given me my instructions. It seems everything's worked out precisely as you've planned it.'

'Not quite,' Jace said softly, reading her like a book. 'I didn't plan on you voting for me.'

'I didn't vote for you,' Tammy lied, a kind of perverse pride making her reluctant to admit the truth.

Jace's mouth formed into a wry grin as he adjusted his stance and placed his hands into his trouser pockets to survey the false picture of deceit on her face. 'Try again,' he prompted gently.

'I really don't know why you must insist on forcing a wrongful admission,' she answered tautly.

'There were only sixteen votes to count,' Jace explained.

'We know that Calvin got seven and I the remaining nine. I did however expect to get eight, suspecting Calvin had bribed five of the members and that he'd receive your vote. It could've been a tie.'

'What - what are you saying?' Tammy asked weakly.

'I'm saying that *yours* was the deciding vote,' Jace concluded. 'And I must admit, I'm at a complete loss as to why you did it.'

Tammy closed her eyes for a moment, Jace's derisive words burning into her soul like acid. She'd done it because she loved him with every fibre of her body and because she'd realised that he was the right candidate to head the company, though she hadn't known just how close a contest it really was.

Keeping her face urbane, she said in a businesslike manner, 'I didn't want you to plan a hostile takeover and sell off our assets for profit, particularly when your talents could be best served increasing the company's turnover.'

Ignoring the gauntlet, Jace asked, 'Was that the only reason?'

No! Tammy's heart yelled painfully. She wanted Jace to know how much she loved him and how she secretly yearned that he loved her in return.

Despite their differences and everything they'd argued and fought about, they had been close and as the days had gone by, she'd developed a burning ache of discontent to feel the strength of his body against hers. At times, it was all she could think about and in her dreams, Tammy had found herself reaching in anguish for him as he appeared before her eyes, then as quickly vanished into the depth of her immagination.

It was on the tip of her tongue to admit to the truth; the words seemed so simple, but they failed to fall from her lips in fear that Jace may reject her. Instead, and as levelly as she could, she said, 'Yes, it is.'

For endless seconds, Jace stared at her numbly, his face a smooth mask of disbelief. Tammy felt her face stiffen with the effort of hiding the misery she refused to let him see. In that moment, she felt a fierce primitive urge to hit out at him for putting her through yet another emotional cyclone, but decided instead to clutch tightly onto her handbag, squeezing her hands with enough pressure to vent the frustration she felt within.

Finally, when he spoke, Tammy sighed inwardly with relief that Jace was not intending to pursue that topic further. 'Will you be alright getting Hattie home from the hospital tomorrow?' he asked mildly.

She nodded. 'I'm going to stay at her house for a few days.'

'That's good,' Jace smiled. He reached into his inner jacket pocket and removed a small card. 'This is my personal telephone number in Brazil,' he said handing her the white card. 'I'll be phoning tomorrow to see how Hattie is, but please call me if there are any changes in her condition.'

'I will,' Tammy agreed. 'Are your parents going back with you?'

'Yes, we leave tonight,' Jace answered solemnly. He sighed then added, 'My mother really liked you.'

Tammy's heart turned sickly as she remembered the task they'd both set for themselves. 'Who knows,' she smiled awkwardly, 'I may meet her again sometime.'

'Who knows,' Jace repeated just as awkward, again feeling that unnamed and unfamiliar emotion wash over him.

'Well,' Tammy swallowed bravely. 'You'd better get back in there and finish your speech.'

'They can wait,' Jace grimaced, placing a hand on her arm. 'Before you go, I just want you to know that I'm sorry I hurt you. Believe me, I never intended to do that.'

'There's no need for you to keep apologising,' Tammy replied, carefully pulling her arm away to deflect the sudden rush of tearful emotion. 'Let's just forget the whole thing ever happened okay?'

She was about to turn and leave when Jace, without warning, took her chin between his fingers and gently raised her face toward him. 'I can't forget,' he whispered, studying her blank, closed expression.

As if hypnotised, Tammy gazed into his strong face so close to hers. A disturbing face that looked as though he was about to lose something of great value. 'Jace, I . . .' Her voice faltered as his face moved nearer.

His smokey brown eyes came into sharp focus, then blurred as he bent his head. Though her heart was flapping about like a trapped butterfly and it was difficult to breathe, Tammy forced herself to remain quite still.

Maybe it was her vulnerability which swayed him, or the fact that Jace suspected that she loved him, but whatever the reason, when his mouth met hers, it was with a totally unexpected sweetness that was as delicious as glaced cherries.

It was the briefest of kisses, yet Jace kissed her deeply, druggingly, engulfing her mouth into his that Tammy's brain clouded and all she was conscious of was Jace and the need he had aroused in her.

When he gently released her, she could see the rigid tension in his powerful shoulders and suddenly became aware that in those three seconds when he'd kissed her, Jace's whole body had tensed with the finality of it. His face was carefully blank, but she saw the desperation in his eyes and his voice, hoarse and tight, spoke with words like they were being wrenched from him.

'Promise me when you tell Hattie,' he said gently, 'that you make it easy for her to understand. I don't want her too upset over the news.'

Determined not to cry, Tammy nodded in mutual agreement and tried to erect a screen of composure to hide behind as Jace turned and strode back toward the boardroom.

Afterward, she took a taxi home and flung off her shoes in front of the sitting room fire. Collapsing into a chair, she suddenly heard the rain begin to fall outside and thought how it reflected the raining tears in her heart.

Jace's face immediately pictured in her head; his thick dark brows, smouldering brown eyes, the cleft in his square chin. Tammy remembered everything about him. When they'd first met, she'd found him strikingly handsome, but rude and had later told him that her life would never be assigned to him. *'Don't speak too soon,'* his words echoed in her head. *'You may just find that you are wholly accountable to me'.*

Her eyes stung with remorse as she closed them. Never were there more truism in such few words spoken.

Suddenly, to Tammy's horror, the tears came tumbling down. She pressed her eyes tightly in an effort to hold them back, but they squeezed themselves beneath her lids and rolled down her cheeks.

It would be a bitter lesson learning how to mend a broken heart, she thought tearfully, but she'd get over it. Just as she would get over Jace Washington.

CHAPTER NINE

TAMMY'S SHOWER cubicle felt like an absolute haven as she turned the shower to a needle spray and allowed the hot water to surge her delicate skin. Scrubbing her face and body, she tried to rid herself of every vestige of Jace Washington.

If only she could get him out of her mind that easily. She'd hardly slept a wink just thinking about him and the way they'd separated.

His abrupt departure had left her abandoned in a kind of emotional limbo and she wondered whether she could ever convince herself that the whole thing had never happened. The answer was simple - she couldn't.

Turning off the shower, she stepped from the cubicle and wrapped herself in a large bath towel. The best thing would be to chalk it up to experience and carry on with her life, Tammy thought, telling herself it would be easy to put Jace completely out of her mind.

In actual practice, it was impossible. She loved Jace and if the past events were to teach her anything, it was the magnitude of love she had to give another human being. Despite the dull ache in her heart spurned by that one thought, Tammy padded slowly into the kitchen and switched on the kettle. She was about to return to her bedroom when there was a sudden knock at her front door. It was a welcome relief, if only to detach her from the moody euphoria to which she had submerged herself.

Placing a smile to her face reserved for such persons as the milkman or postman, she twisted a towel around her hair and padded across the hallway to open the front door.

The worried face that greeted her with a weak smile raised Tammy's bravado immediately. 'Sherelle!' she said drily, but startled nonetheless.

'I have to talk to you,' Sherelle said earnestly. 'Can I come in?'

'I don't know,' Tammy replied coolly, folding her arms beneath her breast to accenuate her acute displeasure at seeing the other woman. 'I was about to get dressed.'

Normally, Tammy liked her own sex. She'd never regarded other women as rivals or potential enemies, even though she didn't go along with sisterhood either, but Sherelle Tate was a definite threat and her better side stood guard, braced for trouble.

'I know it's a real imposition having me barge in on you like this,' Sherelle apologised, 'especially after my behaviour the last time we spoke, but it's very important.'

Tammy quietly spread the door open and stepped aside. 'You'd better come in then.' She led the way toward the kitchen and invited Sherelle to sit down before adding, 'I was about to make some tea. You look like you could do with a cup.'

'Yes, thank you,' Sherelle accepted mildly.

Tammy filled two cups and carried them to the small breakfast table. Taking her seat opposite the older woman, she picked her way carefully. 'Is there a problem you think I can help you with?'

Sherelle bent her head over her cup. 'It's Calvin,' she said in a low voice.

Tammy made a sound of annoyance. She had expected the problem to be Jace. 'Is *that* all?'

Sherelle raised her head in surprise. 'I wish it was,' she answered overly concerned. 'I'm worried about him. Aren't you?'

'Calvin can take good care of himself,' Tammy countered before sipping her tea. 'He's renowned for that.'

'Haven't you noticed how much he's been drinking

lately?' Sherelle persisted.   'I heard about the board decision yesterday and what happened afterward and . . .'

'When you get to know Calvin better,' Tammy interrupted drily, swirling the hot tea around in her cup, 'you'll discover that the only person he cares about is himself.   Don't take it personally, but the fact that he singled you out the moment you arrived in England is something which comes naturally to him.'

Sherelle leaned back into her chair, her eyes blazing. 'Well I'm glad about that,' she commented sternly, 'otherwise we would never have met had it not been for him asking me to come here in the first place.'

Tammy's hazel eyes sliced over Sherelle's vulnerable flowerlike face in total comprehension of the apparent change in the other woman which she knew mirrored the somewhat similar change in herself.

'As I don't know you any better,' she said in a matter of fact way, 'I can only hazard a guess that you're falling in love.'

Sherelle's lips curled pretentiously.   'Maybe I am, I don't know. I'm still trying to come to grips with what I'm going through.'

'You and Calvin,' Tammy drawled the words slowly. 'I thought . . .'

'I know,' Sherelle nodded, a flash of humour lighting her strained face.   'I got thrown off track after the charity function and everything just, clicked into place. You understand.'

Did she?   Tammy wondered whether she'd ever understood anything at all. The only thing she was certain of in her mind was her love for Jace and the attempt she must make to repair the damage done between them before it was too late.

'I know we have our differences,' Sherelle continued regardless of Tammy's wandering attention, 'but Calvin needs your help. I think you ought to talk to him.'

'He's . . . uh . . . he's at home then?' Tammy forcefully

jolted her attention back to Sherelle.

'Yes, but he won't let anyone into the apartment,' Sherelle said with worry. 'Will you go and see him today?'

'I'm expected to pick up my grandmother from the hospital at one o'clock,' Tammy answered lightly, 'but since you insist, I'll go over to Calvin's as soon as I'm dressed.'

Sherelle pushed her chair back. 'Thank you,' she said gratefully. 'Will you please ask him to call me?'

Tammy nodded.

'There is just one other thing,' Sherelle prompted when they reached the front door. 'I didn't mean it about the divorce settlement, but I heard about that too. Girl, I hope it works out for you. Marry the man today and change his ways tomorrow, that's my motto. Good luck.'

After she'd left, Tammy rinsed out the cups and thought of the wisdom behind Sherelle's words. Being an older and more experienced woman, she guessed Sherelle was an authority on affairs of the heart. It was hard to believe though that after the trouble Sherelle had made over Jace that she could've harboured such deep feelings for Calvin and she wondered curiously whether Calvin had any similar feelings to give in return.

Her mind immediately jilted that idea. She couldn't imagine Calvin caring about anyone except himself, but being his kid sister, she felt obligated to give him the moral support he needed presently, even though it would probably just inflate his self-centred ego.

Catching a cab, Tammy leaned heavily against the back seat and instructed the driver to her destination. Her brother's troubles had been a good detour for most of the morning, giving her the blessed period she needed to obliterate Jace from her thoughts. But now he was back in full force and she didn't welcome the sudden memory of Jace's darkly handsome face and compelling male body.

Rubbing her temple as though she had a headache, Tammy mentally cursed him for walking into her life and turning it upside down. Why in God's name did she ever allow him to do it?

Surely her grandmother would've recovered her recent setback without the pretense of a family wedding, she thought furiously. After all, she'd survived two such previous attacks.

She was willing to believe that Jace had an ulterior motive, that he found her just as attractive as she'd found him and that was the reason behind his assimilation of their romance. She was even willing to believe that her grandmother's illness had nothing to do with it, but deep down, she knew that was wishful thinking.

Jace Washington had no intentions of dating her let alone meeting her. When her grandmother had recovered her stroke, he couldn't wait to get away, grateful that he need never spend another moment with her. Yet he'd kissed her, shattering every fibre in her body with the power of it. He'd even insisted that she keep the ring until he returned from Brazil, suggesting that they should talk afterward.

Tammy wondered what his possible reason could be. Did he still expect to be rewarded for his efforts by sharing her bed, or did he have a more amicable parting in mind? She didn't dare guess, though she reminded herself how badly he'd wanted to make love to her.

During their short time together, he'd presumed his rights to her body and affections, making every endeavour to tempt her amorously and she'd been tempted; tempted enough to allow him to strip her naked. She would've given herself too, wholly and without resignation had he not degraded her with the implication that her virginity was an old fashioned virtue that needed to be rid of.

Fury and pain blazed through her in recollection and she angrily jerked her mind away from those thoughts and concentrated on the traffic that glided by. It was a good diversion, easing the torment that concurred in her mind.

Ten minutes later, the taxi pulled up alongside two

other cars and the driver beckoned to her that she had arrived at her destination.

Tammy instructed him to wait as she only expected to breeze into Calvin's penthouse for a fleeting visit then breeze right out again after ascertaining that he was fine. She imagined that he would be.

Besides, she told herself by way of persuasion, she was already short for time, having packed a small suitcase, her next stop scheduled for the hospital and then directly to her grandmother's house where she would be staying for the duration.

Stepping from the elevator car, Tammy walked the short distance to Calvin's door and rung the doorbell twice. There was no answer. She tried again, this time ringing several times. Still there was no answer. Finally, she hammered a firm, hard knock with her knuckles and then again with the palm of her hand. 'Calvin, it's me, Tammy,' she yelled, a little concerned. 'I know you're in there. Let me in.'

There was a moment of silence then Tammy heard Calvin's heavy footsteps seconds before the lock clicked back and the door opened quietly. 'Calvin?'

'What do you want?' Calvin slurred, squinting his eyes against the light that shone through from the corridor window.

'I came to see if you were alright,' Tammy said a little alarmed at his appearance. He was unshaven, stenched of beer and was still dressed in his pyjamas though it was already gone 12.30 in the day. 'I see you haven't gone into work then.'

'What work?' Calvin scoffed, allowing the door to swing open as he turned toward the lounge, uncaring whether Tammy followed him there or not. 'Haven't you heard? Oh, but of course, you haven't,' he sneered treacherously. 'You left before I gained consciousness. Well, for your information, I've been demoted to a job that holds only a menial capacity of what I'm accustomed to, you've been replaced with someone who really knows about cosmetic packaging, - she's redesigning the entire Ebon range, and your lover is now considering a merger, but what do you care? You've already resigned after stabbing me in the back.'

'Calvin, I . . .'

'Save it sis,' her brother blazed, expelling a hiccough. 'You and our darling grandmother both. I was so close. It would've been a tie you know. I only needed one vote to win, another would've been nice for comfort, but my own family whose two votes would've clinched my inheritance, kicks me in the guts.'

Tammy's heart twisted, agonising her brother's pain, but she refused nonetheless to allow him to make her feel guilty over a decision she knew to be right for the company. 'I'm sorry you feel that way,' she answered calmly, willing him to understand. 'But you know as well as I do that you would never have done that job properly nor what the board of directors wanted. You . . .'

'I would've made damn sure that the company stayed in our hands,' Calvin roared. 'Did Jace Washington build you up to this? Did he promise to marry you to compensate for what rightfully belongs to a Caswell?'

'Jace had nothing to do with it,' Tammy shouted in return. 'And I'm sick and tied of you feeling so outdone by, especially when we - Caswells - still jointly own the majority of the company. I made the right decision overall and in hindsight, I did the right thing considering what a fine spectacle you made of yourself yesterday.'

'And in hindsight,' Calvin jeered, 'I should've expected your traitory considering what a fine actress your are. Well I won't forget this. Whilst that man sits in my chair, I'll never forget.'

'I'm leaving,' Tammy said tearfully, deciding to refer from explaining any further. 'You obviously don't need me here to help you wallow in your own self-pity.'

'I see you're still wearing his ring,' Calvin suddenly

jabbed with amazement. 'I'll not have you marry him you know. That bastard doesn't deserve your love.'

Tammy's eyes widened increduously. 'You know that I love him?'

'Jason told me,' Calvin replied drily. 'It's written all over your face too, but you can forget him because by the time he returns from Brazil, plan B will already be in operation.'

Dread and panic coarsed the length of Tammy's body, the fear evident in her voice. 'What - what do you mean?'

'I mean, my dear sister, that Jason Lee is now in the running for your sweet affections. The scandal sheets will probably make a scoop out of it, given a few days and the right information from an insider.'

'You - stupid - idiot,' Tammy yelled, her face hot with the rising heat of her fury and scorn. 'Sherelle Tate must be absolutely mad to feel the way she does about you. Have you any idea what you've done?'

Calvin retreated two steps as though he'd been struck head on.

'Grandma is going to be discharged from the hospital today,' she told him madly. 'If she picks up a newspaper and reads . . .' Tammy couldn't bear to think of the consequences.

Calvin disguised his emotions well, though the wealth of remorse reflected in his eyes. 'You'd better get to her before the press hounds do,' he said silently. 'I'll drive you.'

'I have a taxi waiting,' Tammy chided, already turning on her heels to make her exit. 'You'd better just pray nothing's happened to her, or else.'

She arrived at the hospital as quickly as the traffic permitted, instructing the driver non too tactfully to take the shortest route there. He'd relunctantly obliged, weaving in and out of traffic with the expertise of a rally driver. She'd urged him to work the speedometer, but the fact that they'd made haste in getting there served as no encouragement to her worried mind.

Again, Tammy instructed him to wait, only this time she was riding anxiously in the hospital elevator car, desperate to reach her grandmother before the paparazzi did. Her heart hammered loudly as the elevator doors swung open and her legs took her quickly toward her grandmother's room.

The private ward was filled with voices the moment Tammy arrived there and she found herself fearing the worse, afraid of what she would find when she entered the four window room. Holding her breath, she pushed open the door and rushed in.

'Tammy, you arrive just in the nick of time,' Hattie smiled, watching her grandaughter hurtle forward like a maniac on wheels. 'The doctor just give me the all clear.'

Tammy eyed the consultant and two nurses suspiciously, her mistrusting mind suspecting that they were probably journalists in disguise. 'You're - you're okay then?' she eventually stammered, frantically scanning the room for the slightest evidence of a newspaper. She saw none and could only assume that Hattie hadn't found the time that morning to take any interest in them.

She wasn't even sure whether there was any commentary based on the falsified information Calvin had circulated, but she felt bound nonetheless to take whatever precautions she could, at least until she'd perused the papers herself.

'Of course me alright,' Hattie reassured.

'She'll be fine,' the consultant reinforced warmly. 'Provided she has plenty of rest and take these.' Tammy was handed a small bottle of pills. 'They'll ease the pain she's suffered from the slight paralysis,' the consultant explained. 'She has very little movement in her left arm, so I'd like to see her at clinic in two weeks. In the meantime, I don't want her excited or working,' he stressed.

'I'll make sure she doesn't so much as read the financial pages,' Tammy promised.

'Let's go home,' Hattie smiled wryly.

The consultant chuckled as they bid their farewells, then Tammy carried the three bunches of flowers and the small suitcase containing Hattie's things to the waiting taxi.

They had no sooner arrived at the car when a formally dressed woman appeared from the middle of nowhere, deliberately wedged herself between Tammy and her grandmother and said quite astutely, 'Would you like to comment on the unfolding situation of your brief relationship with Jace Washington amid current rumours of your rekindled romance with an old flame?'

'No, I would not,' Tammy jabbed rudely, roughly urging her grandmother into the car.

'Is it true then that your jilted lover has left the country to escape the scandal and embarrassment?' the woman persisted.

'I don't know what you're talking about,' Tammy chided firmly, quickly entering the car. 'Mr Washington is away on business. Now get lost and leave us alone.' She slammed the door and tapped the driver's shoulder to move on.

'What that woman a talk 'bout?' Hattie immediately demanded as the taxi surged into the midday traffic. 'What rekindled romance?'

'She's just looking for a story,' Tammy prevaricated with wit. 'You know newspaper reporters. They like to stir up their own ingredients and cook it. When we get home, I'll make you your favourite lunch, goat fish soup.'

'Me long fe taste that,' Hattie smiled.

The driver made up for the time he'd lost rushing to the hospital by taking the cruise journey toward Hattie's home. Tammy welcomed the slow progression, her mind thinking carefully on the tactics she could employ to avoid her grandmother from reading a newspaper.

It was obvious from the reporter they'd collided with that the news was already travelling and Tammy knew that she would be unable to keep it from her grandmother for very long.

'You quiet,' Hattie broke into her troubled thoughts. 'You a miss Jace?'

Tammy cast her eyes sideways and felt her mouth go superdry. 'I . . .'

'No mind,' Hattie prompted, giving her grandaughter's hand a little squeeze. 'He'll be back soon. We have plenty of time to sort out the wedding arrangements.'

Tammy's face looked cane pale as the blood drained out of her cheeks. There was still the broken engagement which she had yet to tell Hattie about. Doubled with the rumour Calvin had invented, nothing could be more potent than the present cocktail for disaster.

Under the circumstances, there was no possible way she could break the news to her grandmother that there would be no wedding and that in turn meant only one thing, everything would have to remain scheduled as planned.

'Tammy, wha' wrong?' Hattie remarked concerned.

Thrown off balance by her grandmother's sudden observation, Tammy sought for a light answer. 'It would be nice if Calvin could give me away,' she muffled without thinking.

Seeing her emotion, Hattie smiled. 'Leave Calvin to me.'

Little did her grandmother know that her frantic emotion was not for Calvin, but for Jace and the loveless marriage she may ultimately have to force him into if she couldn't curtail Calvin's rumour in time.

The telephone was ringing loudly the moment Tammy and her grandmother stepped into the empty, detached house. Tammy deposited the two suitcases onto the parquet floor and urged her grandmother to put the flowers into water whilst she answered the telephone.

She expected it to be Calvin, desperate to make amends, or perhaps one of her grandmother's brigade of friends from the church Hattie sometimes frequented, but the second she heard Jace's deep baritone asking for Mama

Hattie, Tammy's heart stopped and her breath came up in little gasps of hurried anticipation. 'Jace!' Her voice sounded weak.

'Hello Tammy,' Jace answered with a calmness that infuriated her. It was obvious from his tone that he was totally unaffected by the sound of her voice as she was from his. 'How are you?'

'I'm - fine,' she replied with a sudden polite manner which she hoped would give her strength.

'And Hattie?'

'She's home and she's fine too.'

'That's wonderful,' Jace said with good natured mirth. 'I wanted to be sure that you managed to get her home. Will you give her my love?'

'Of course,' Tammy assured, secretly wishing he would give her his love too.

She was wondering what to say next, or whether she should say anything at all when he asked, 'How are things?'

Recalling the kind of morning she'd had first with Sherelle and Calvin, and then with a member of the press, she said simply, 'Here and there.'

'Mostly where?' Jace prodded, detecting something in her voice.

Tammy wondered where she should start. She knew he had to be told about Calvin's latest escapade, but she feared her grandmother overhearing the conversation. Worse, she feared Jace's reaction on discovering that their pretense would have to go on for a little longer.

So instead, she answered lightly, 'Mostly at home.'

'Calvin,' Jace immediately surmised with an accuracy that shook her. 'Has he been taking his misery out on you?'

'He's just a little overwrought,' Tammy declared, keeping her voice reasonably low. 'Please don't worry about it.'

'Well call me the minute he becomes a problem,' Jace told her firmly. 'I have a notion he's going to start something.'

Tammy stared mutely at the telephone, too breathless to speak. Calvin had already started something, she thought fearful of Jace's sixth sense of judgement. If he were ever to know that he was rumoured to have had left the country to momentarily save himself the embarrassment of being jilted, Calvin wouldn't see his guts for garters.

She knew it was down to her to avoid that kind of confrontation. She would wait until he arrived back from Brazil and then rationalise Calvin's conduct in a tactful and unemotive manner. That way, she could keep a clear head when she told him that they were still, for the time being, destined to marry.

'Tammy, are you still there?' Jace's voice broke her trancelike state.

'Yes - yes,' she muffled, jolting her senses quickly.

Jace's voice softened. 'You're worried over something.'

'I'm fine,' she insisted.

'I take it you haven't told Hattie yet?' he said hesitantly.

Tammy's heart sank. 'No.' The word was barely audible. There was a short silence at the other end. Tammy felt an acute sense of loss, of rejection and briefly, her composure slipped a notch, revealing the misery beneath her already worried mask. 'I don't think I should rush into it,' she added weakly.

'Then don't,' Jace told her gently. 'Don't try and handle it by yourself.' It was an order and he meant it to be obeyed.

'But you said . . .'

'I know what I said,' Jace interrupted, slightly irritated at her protest of his authoritative stance. 'It can wait until I get back.'

Emboldened by his manner, Tammy said in a rush with a husky attractive laugh deliberately feigned to disguise her true feelings, 'You sound like you miss me.' It was only after she'd said it, that she wondered where on earth she got the courage.

'Maybe I do at that,' Jace answered bemused. 'Do you realise that in all the time I've known you, that's the first time I've ever heard you laugh?'

Tammy's heart slammed into her ribcage.

'It's a shame I'm not there to see it,' Jace continued in the same tone. 'It would've given me a more pleasant picture to remember you by.'

'I wasn't all that bad,' she defended, hurt by his impression of her. 'Maybe if you hadn't been so demanding then . . .'

'All my actions were in the best interest of everyone concerned,' Jace interrupted. 'Surely you must've realised that by now?'

'I . . .'

'And,' Jace pressed. 'If I hadn't been so demanding as you put it, then Hattie would most likely still be in hospital right now.'

It was true, Tammy thought wryly, despite her and her brother's scheming and somewhat lame attempts at preventing him from ever being involved in their lives. She should be grateful for all he'd done and deep down she was, Tammy told herself ruefully. For not only had Jace obligated himself to the care and wellbeing of her grandmother, but he'd taken care of the company too, securing its future at the cost of upsetting others and unselfishly forcing himself into an engagement as a protection measure.

It was a chain of responsibility many a man would've rejected, she thought logically, but Jace had accepted it with his brand of dignity and strength, and perhaps, she mused, with the challenge of controlling her openly defiant nature.

'I guess I owe you an apology,' she found herself saying with a sincere note of affection. 'I haven't been easy have I? You can admit it.'

'No you haven't,' Jace confirmed softly, 'but you've got

me totally baffled and that's a more amazing admission than you'll ever realize.'

There was a quality to his low voice that stirred a delicious shiver right through to Tammy's nerve endings. Did that mean Jace felt something for her besides and beyond the fact that he cared? Tammy couldn't be sure, nor did she even dare hope.

For in the time she'd known him, not once had Jace opened the door to his mind, or revealed the slightest indication to his inner thoughts. If only he'd let her know what he was really thinking, then she could be certain. Certain that there was hope for him to love her.

With that in mind, Tammy decided to toss a little mystique in return for the enigmatic composure Jace had always presented to her. 'Maybe you ought to get to know me a little better,' she said silky.

'Maybe I should at that,' Jace answered as though he meant it.

'But be warned,' Tammy cautioned with a smile. 'Baffled men often fall in love.'

'Do they now?' Jace chuckled, more as a statement than in query. 'Then I look forward to the prospect of breaking down those barriers you've erected.'

Choosing to savour his suggestive remark, Tammy instead tackled, 'I'm your relunctant significant other remember?'

She sensed the grin in Jace's cheeky reply as his voice deepened with sensuality. 'I'm going to have to do something about that.'

Tammy's heart warmed with a glow of happiness. Jace had once said he had no intentions of seducing her, yet here he was, doing precisely that and she was loving every minute of it. Firmly deciding to indulge in his provocative teasing, she opened her mouth ready to toss out another remark, when Hattie's voice intervened in speculation.

'Tammy, who is that on the phone? Is it Calvin?'

'It's Jace,' Tammy called in return.

Her disappointment at the intrusion was eclipsed when Hattie rushed out of the kitchen and into the hallway. 'Let me speak to him,' she enthused, immediately seizing the telephone. 'Jace my boy, how are you?'

Tammy stood next to her grandmother and listened intently to the brief conversation that went on for five minutes. Hattie talked excitedly about the plans she had in mind for their wedding and how happy she was to be out of the hospital. Finally, totally exhausted from the chit chat, she handed Tammy back the telephone. 'Jace wants a quick word before he goes.' Hattie sounded tied. 'Me a go lie down.'

'Grandma, are you alright?' Tammy asked, her eyebrows raised in acute alarm.

'Yes Tammy, no fuss,' Hattie answered in irritation. 'Me going to me room.'

Tammy watched as her grandmother slowly took the stairs to her room then quickly directed her attention to the phone. Jace was already calling her name. 'Tammy, is everything okay?'

'Yes - I think,' she said a little unsure.

'Look, I'm scheduled to be at a meeting in two minutes, so I have to go, but I'm here if you need me. Remember that.'

'I will.'

As she replaced the receiver, Tammy mulled over Jace's last words. *'I'm here if you need me.'* The joy and security she felt from them was overwhelming. Jace loved her, she dreamed with hazy eyes and she loved him. In that perfect world of inner peace and profound contentment, she thought of nothing but the man whose destiny lied with her.

CHAPTER TEN

TAMMY AWOKE the following morning to the sound of rain beating against the windows. Feeling a little disorientated, she turned onto her side and then dazily looked around the unfamiliar room.

It was a while before she realised where she was and in doing so, the thought jolted her out of bed in an instant. Hattie normally had her morning paper delivered she thought frantically, silently applauding herself for the way she'd yesterday discreetly seized the latest paper lying among the small pile of mail and dated newspapers.

Hattie had gone to bed and had therefore not seen her frantic motion. Now, hectically grabbing her nightgown, she flung open the bedroom door and rushed out into the hall then down the stairs.

Fortunately, that morning's newspaper was still on the front door mat. Quickly placing it beneath her nightgown, she tiptoed up the stairs and back into her bedroom. Hopefully, her grandmother hadn't heard her, Tammy sighed wearily, her fingers already flicking through the paper with speed.

At first, she didn't see anything of interest. Then her heart sank with dread as her eyes spotted the single column article neatly cornered at the bottom of page seven. There were no photographs, but it was clear in which direction the coverage had intended to lead its reader. It read:

'JACE P WASHINGTON JR, JILTED LOVER AND NEWLY APPOINTED CHAIRMAN OF CASWELL COSMETICS, WAS CONDEMNED YESTERDAY AS A

CONNIVING PROFIT HUSSLER AND CONFIDENCE TRICKSTER.'

'THE ATTACK CAME FROM CASWELL COSMETIC'S MARKETING DIRECTOR, JASON LEE, WHO HAS RECENTLY REPLACED THE SPURNED LOVER IN YOUNG MISS CASWELL'S AFFECTIONS.'

Tammy immediately closed the paper. She didn't want to read anymore. She felt nothing but fury over the entire matter.

The only thing she could imagine would stamp out Calvin's ridiculous story was by her speaking to a reporter, she thought, loathing the very idea. But if there were any other way of justifying her integrity, not to mention Jace's pride as well as maintain her grandmother's present stability at one and the same time, she couldn't think of it.

She shuddered to think what possible information Calvin could've leaked for it seemed strange to her that Jason Lee should speak out so openly about a rumour that should rightly have died a natural death.

Slowly, relentlessly, fear began to uncoil its silky tendrils in her stomach. It wasn't possible that Calvin and Jason would contest Jace's sovereignty, as Calvin had put it, to the company. Surely not. But the more Tammy thought about it, the more it seemed possible.

She clapsed her trembling hands together, thinking quickly. She should call Jace and warn him, her mind told her firmly. He would have a solution; he would know what to do. But deep down, she didn't want to disturb the beautiful rapport they'd built up the day before.

For the first time since their meeting of each other, they'd talked like two companions, their conversation bridging on amusement, spontaneous teasing and punctuated with the kind of sexual inneundo she found titillating. Tammy wanted to hold onto that moment forever, but in reality, she knew she could only hold onto it until Jace returned.

Only then would she feel ready to explain the reports in

the newspapers. Until that time, she thought ruefully, she would continue her endeavours in keeping the papers away from her grandmother.

A HARSH jangling noise finally succeeded in waking Tammy from her bliss of deep sleep. At first she buried her nose in the pillow until all that was visible was a cloud of cascading black hair.

When the sound refused to go away, she opened her drowsy eyes. The bedside clock said it was almost 7.30 am, but it wasn't the alarm that woke her. Tammy scowled at the telephone, but it wasn't the inoffensive instrument that was ringing either. Suddenly, she realised that it was the doorbell downstairs.

Donning her nightgown, she rubbed her eyes and began the slow pursuit downstairs. She clasped her nightgown around her waist and then proceeded toward the front door. Who could possibly be calling at such an hour? she thought wretchedly, as she swung open the door. Tammy's body instantly froze in shock as Jace, clad in a long black cashmere coat, stalked in out of the cold morning air.

Ten days had passed since they'd last seen each other, although to Tammy, it felt like she'd been on tenderhooks for an eternity. Jace was scheduled to return in four days, and luckily for her, she'd expertly managed to keep the gossip-ridden newspapers away from her grandmother.

On one occasion, she'd even been tempted to call Jace and had actually succeeded in dialing his number in Brazil, but when she'd heard his deep baritone voice, her nerves forced her to hang up the telephone. Tammy couldn't explain the circumstances long distance or her feelings on how much she'd missed Jace. And she'd missed him dreadfully.

Now he was here. But when she saw the reckless glitter in his enigmatic brown eyes, her mind screamed a poignant warning. Jace knew about Calvin's ridiculous story to the press.

'Close the door,' he commanded softly. His voice sounded strange and there was an iron grimness in the set of his jaw.

'Why - why aren't you still in Brazil?' Tammy shivered, closing the door as he'd instructed.

'Have you missed me?' Jace countered with a question of his own, his eyes settling on her frazzled face.

Tammy felt as though he had stripped her bare as Jace's eyes bore into her very soul. She tried to think quickly, but couldn't. Her mind was more aware of his tense and angry expression, but he wasn't furious, she told herself logically. Relaxing with that thought, she decided that he must have come all the way from Brazil because he was ready to have their 'talk' now.

With a modest smile tugging at her lips in an attempt to appear coy, she said, 'I've been busy.'

'Busy?' Jace repeated. He walked into the living room sensing that Tammy had followed him there and stood next to the feature fireplace, his elbow propped casually against the mantelpiece.

For a long moment Jace charted the mess of uncombed hair resting heavily on Tammy's shoulders then travelled downward past her acutely alarmed expression to the shimmering pale blue nightdress that revealed the delicate curves of her body.

Tammy didn't like his blatant study of her, nor the disturbing way in which he did it, but her heart warmed when Jace's gaze shifted to her innocent face and he whispered silky, 'I've missed you.'

'Is - is that why you came back early?' she asked shakily, unsure whether she should believe her own ears.

Ignoring her question, Jace invited smoothly, 'Come here.'

Tammy obediently walked the metre and a half toward him, suppressing the overpowering urge to rush directly into Jace's arms. When she was within a foot of him, he reached out and caught her wrist, gently pulling her into his warm embrace.

For an instant, she sensed a stiffening in his shoulders that sent an unexplainable bell of alarm to ring in her head. Her timorous mind was on the brink of deciphering it when Jace's deep voice commanded softly, 'Kiss me.'

Tammy stared into the steely brown eyes that suddenly seemed to soften at her gaze. She didn't know what to make of him, or the disturbing combination of desire and unusual restraint that spread like a warning rash along her body. It was only as Jace crushed her slender body to the rigid, contours of his own did she decide to throw caution to the wind.

'Kiss me,' his voice repeated hoarsely above her lips. 'You do want to kiss me?'

Tammy's brows rose in surprise. She thought she'd been the only one with insecurities, but it was plainly obvious to her now that Jace had them too. She knew a part of him was holding back, braced for her answer of rejection. He'd missed her and he wanted her and now he was waiting to see if she wanted him.

In that moment, Tammy loved him more than ever. She didn't know whether to hug him, cry, or burst out laughing with the surpreme joy of knowing that Jace loved her. For that was what every fibre in her body divulged to her vulnerable mind.

Sliding her hands up his hardened muscular chest to the curve of his shoulders, she whispered against his lips, 'Your kisses are all I ever dream about.'

Tammy felt the tremor that ran through Jace's body the instant their lips joined. Jace kissed her fiercely, temptuously and still he couldn't get enough of her. When her lips parted, his tongue slipped between them for a sweet arousing taste of her hunger for him. He retreated and hungrily plunged again, this time in a tormenting gesture intent to tease.

Tammy tried to restrain the exploding passion that engulfed her, but lost all control. Instead, she snuggled closer to the warmth of Jace's cashmere coat, returning his kiss with an intensity totally new to her quivering nervous system.

She took his gasps of shuddering excitement into her mouth, enjoying them with the fierce delight of a woman in love. Yet somewhere among the turmult of her whirling senses, Tammy realised that Jace's kiss had altered.

Though he was sensuously moving his lips to tell her of his raging passion, his pattern had changed. She felt as though he'd begun to handle her like a baker would a familiar piece of dough. At first, he had been as desperate for her as she was for him, uncontrolled, wayward. Now, he was restrained, skilled, every brush of his lips intent on inflaming her passion.

And he'd succeeded. Desire was racing through her like wild fire by the time Jace dragged his mouth away and held her so that she could physically feel his pounding heart.

Fighting down the rampaging demands of her own body, Tammy pulled back into his arms and lifted her eyes to his, expectant to see them reflecting the same twinkle of love as her own. Instead, there were furrows between Jace's brows and his expression was bridged on an accusation.

'What is it?' she immediately queried, hearing the alarm bells again in her head.

'Is it true?'

'Is what true?'

'About you and Jason Lee?'

Tammy's eyes widened in disbelief. He'd known, she thought suddenly in mounting surprise. He'd known all along. That was why he came back to England, not because he loved her, but because his traitorous mind believed the scandal covered in the newspapers. She didn't have time to ponder how he came by the information, only to think quickly how she would explain what caused the circumstance to arise.

'Is it true?' Jace's menacing voice demanded again.

'No it isn't,' Tammy cried out. 'I wanted to explain . . .'

'I'm sure you did,' Jace rudely interrupted, releasing her with the same venom.

'Please let me explain,' Tammy implored, telling herself that she should remain calm, though it was difficult with the murderous glare on Jace's face which had already convicted her guilty. 'Calvin decided to fabricate a story about me and Jason to the newspapers. He thought . . .'

'Now why would he do that?' Jace jeered scathingly.

Tammy feverishly tried to explain. 'It was his foolish idea of wreaking revenge,' she began quickly. 'He masqueraded the whole thing to discredit you and punish me for not giving him my vote.'

Jace stood silent for a while, looking into her face with elevated scorn. Tammy's eyes begged that he believe her. Jace knew her brother and what he was capable of, so she couldn't imagine why he was finding it so hard to accept her version of events.

She was soon provided with the answer when Jace pulled a folded piece of newspaper from his cashmere coat pocket and opened it before her very eyes. It was a copy of that morning's paper. 'Then I suppose you'd better explain this to me,' his steely voice demanded. 'I tore it from a paper I happened to buy at the airport.'

Tammy stared in paralysed terror at the two year old photograph of her and Jason Lee, locked in a tender embrace and evidently kissing. The caption read:
'LIPS SEALED AS SECRET TWO YEAR ROMANCE BREAKS'
The story went on to indicate her as having carried on a sordid affair with Jason before and throughout her engagement to Jace. The affair was cited as the underlying cause of their breakup and Jace was hinted to have had *'gone away on vacation'* to escape the scandal prior to taking up his post at Caswell Cosmetics where he would, no doubt, be working alongside his *'enemy in love'*.

Tammy felt her mouth go superdry, but she met the deadly glare in Jace's eyes nonetheless. 'This - this picture isn't what it seems,' she stuttered desperately.

Jace's eyes flashed with a blazing orange light under peaked eyebrows that were drawn together in a ferocious scowl of disbelief. 'Isn't it?' he quipped in a deadly tone. 'On the contrary, I'd say it was very tangible evidence to the truth.'

'That picture happens to be two years old,' Tammy explained lamely, her mind spinning the sequence of events which had led to that fateful kiss. It was Christmas Eve and Jason had caught her under a mistletoe as she'd entered Calvin's kitchen preparatory to making coffee.

She'd drunk a little more than her usual quota, so when Jason had asked her in such a polite manner for a kiss, she'd stupidly obligated his proposal. She'd offered it in the party spirit in which it was intended, but it later became apparent to her that Jason had taken it differently.

'So, you didn't turn down his passes after all,' Jace accused disgustedly. 'Did you date him?'

'No,' Tammy answered quickly. 'I've only kissed Jason once - that was it - at a Christmas Eve party Calvin held at his penthouse two years ago. Someone must've taken a picture when it happened. That's the honest truth, I swear.'

'I'm always wary of people who swear to the truth when they don't acutally confess to it prior to being confronted,' Jace sneered.

'I didn't tell you beforehand,' Tammy declared nervously, 'because I always find that when I preempt a man's reaction, I'm always wrong.'

'I would've behaved in precisely the same manner,' Jace scolded, refusing to accept her excuse. 'Perhaps a little more forgiving because you would've been honest.'

'You would've acted like a tyrant and given the press a field day,' Tammy accused, defending her action not to have told him until he returned from Brazil. 'Not to mention what you would've done to Calvin.'

'Tammy,' Jace bellowed in a dangerously low voice.

'Calvin now believes he can get away with anything and as for the press, they're already lapping it up like spilt milk. So just when were you planning to let me know, after they'd established that you'd slept with Jason Lee?'

Tammy gasped. 'I haven't.'

'Isn't that what I'm supposed to believe?'

Tammy's self restraint snapped along with her steady and forcefully calm composure. 'I'm beside myself justifying to you the truth when you obviously don't want to hear it,' she averred furiously, 'so you can damn well believe what you please.'

She was about to turn on her heels and leave the room when Jace caught her wrist and tightened his grip around it. 'I'd have believed anything of you if it wasn't for your immaculate acting ability,' he said heavily.

Tammy's fury rose. 'What?'

'You've lived up to the assimilation of our romance better than I could ever have hoped,' Jace jeered. 'Infact, at times, I could've sworn you were putting your whole heart and soul into the part. Just tell me one thing, when I kissed you just now, was that for real?'

The hard contempt on Jace's face softened slightly as he searched her expression. Various emotions struggled for supremacy inside Tammy - disbelief, rage, uncertainty and a dawning hope. Hope that Jace would see the love in her eyes. Yet she knew Jace was blind to everything; Calvin's guise of deception, the knowledge that she was still a virgin, and certainly to the fact that she loved him.

He'd kissed her with the thought of degrading her. To build up her desire and then expose her for the pretense and faithlessness he'd accused her guilty of. Now he was seeking her confirmation to that very suspicion.

Her chin lifted in silent rebellion. 'Do you really think I could mask my feelings that well?'

Jace released her wrist and stepped backward, facing Tammy squarely with his face unusually blank. 'Yes I do.'

Totally aghast by his admission, Tammy's only thought

was to exact equal bitter punishment. 'In that case,' she told Jace raggedly, the pain of his words twisting like a sharp blade in her gut. 'Calvin must be right. He said I was a good actress.'

She saw the painful strain in Jace's face and watched as he just as quickly fought it down. 'Then I look forward to seeing your best performance,' he quipped, behaving as though he had been totally unfrazzled by her remark. 'I hope you have no problems reciting your lines.'

Tammy looked at him uncomprehendingly. 'What on earth are you talking about?'

'I've brought the wedding date forward,' Jace declared with a curling satisfaction of his lips. 'Whether you like it or not, we're going to be married.'

Tammy laughed harshly. 'You must be mad to think I would ever marry you. What point would there be in belonging to a man who hates me?'

Jace replied with a raging kind of calm that made her tremble. 'The fact that you could never belong to anybody else.'

Tammy shook her head, unbelieving. 'Why are you doing this?'

'Because I'll not be ridiculed or branded in the press by a feeble, spineless wimp like Jason Lee,' Jace remarked.

'So this is about your pride and ego,' Tammy jabbed flatly. 'Well, for one thing, we're in England not Brazil, and for another, I can't imagine that you'll ever get an earlier wedding date than July 5th.'

'I already have,' Jace confirmed wryly. 'When Randall Garvey called me in Brazil two days ago and asked me if I knew what the papers were saying, I immediately had him ring round the registry offices and book the nearest available date. Westminster Registry Office had a cancellation, so we were lucky.'

'I don't particularly feel lucky,' Tammy boomed.

'You will on the wedding night,' Jace promised, 'so you may just as well get used to the idea.'

A ripple of fear danced along Tammy's spine. 'I'll not be preyed upon by you,' she tossed scornfully. 'I'm no longer obligated to you remember. Our deal of pretense to keep my grandmother happy is over. I even offered to give you your ring back. So you can take it right . . .'

'What was that?' Jace's firm clipped voice cut her midstream.

There had been a noise, like that of a body slumping to the ground. Tammy had heard it too. It sounded like it had come from the entrance hall.

'You wait here,' Jace ordered. He left the room and immediately rushed back seconds later, his face as pale as cane. 'Call an ambulance, quickly.'

'Oh my god, what is it?'

'It's Hattie. I think she's fainted.'

'THIS IS all your fault,' Tammy muttered bitterly beneath her breath as she sat anxiously in the hospital reception. She felt her anxiety rise and clenched her fingers to quell the overwhelming sensation of suffocation. 'If you hadn't come back today, this would never have happened.'

Jace offered her a cup of dispenser coffee and took the seat next to her. 'Here, you need a stimulant,' he said abruptly, 'not that it'll make any difference to your present state of mind.'

'I'm beside myself with worry,' Tammy spat, trying to still the tremble in her legs. 'She must've heard us arguing about the wedding.'

'When I found her,' Jace said in a low aggressive tone, 'she had this morning's newspaper in her hand. My guess is that she saw the picture of you and Jason Lee, only it hit her more dramatically than it hit me.'

'Oh no,' Tammy's voice was ultra weak. 'I didn't hear the paperboy arrive at the door. If you hadn't distracted me . . .'

'So, you were also hiding the truth from Hattie,' Jace interrupted coldly. It wasn't a question, more a statement of fact. 'That's a turn up for the books. You're more deceitful than I would have given you credit for.'

'I was trying to prevent another relapse,' Tammy reasoned weakly, desperately fighting the fear that had begun to surface her anxiety.

'Evidently, you've precipitated it,' Jace clipped in response.

Tammy rose from her seat, the coffee shaking in her hand and her hazel eyes glazed with tears, but she silently resolved not to display any signs of weakness. 'There's only one person who's heightened the tension in everybody's guts and that's you,' she cried loudly. 'Your idea to get married has caused nothing but trouble.'

'On the contrary,' Jace bellowed, raising himself from his own seat just as fast. 'Our engagement has been the one thing that has kept your grandmother happy these past few weeks and her present condition is all the more reason why we're going to be married on Saturday.'

'Saturday?' Tammy's voice fell by two octaves. 'This Saturday?'

'Didn't I tell you?' Jace's voice was cold. 'How rude of me.'

'You - you haven't got the marriage licence,' Tammy stammered in shock.

'I've already picked that up,' Jace reminded. 'I decided after the board meeting that I'd still go and get it, just in case.'

'In case of what? That I would decide to marry you?' Tammy's mind raced for an excuse to abandon the very idea. 'I can't see you getting any witnesses at such short notice, not unless you were to handpick them from the street.'

Jace's lips twisted as though he found that possibility amusing. 'I actually considered that,' he declared mildly, 'but Marchi's flying over from Trinidad, and I think it only right that your brother be there.'

Tammy felt her rage momentarily subside. Jace thought

he had everything organised; his sister as one witness, the date arranged and the assumption that she would be there, but there was Calvin to get over and that thought brought a quirking tug of victory to her lips. 'Calvin would never consent to attend,' she jabbed triumphantly.

'You're forgetting something,' Jace said calmly. Too calm. 'Calvin loves the smell of power. I need only dangle the executive vice president's job under his nose to be assured of his loyal allegiance and support.'

That was true, Tammy's mind conceded, totally defeated and knowing that Calvin would more than willingly accept Jace's offer. What other excuses were there that she could fight with? None. She loved Jace and deep down she wanted to belong to him, but he didn't love her.

That thought hammered against her brain and burrowed into her mind with such severity that she hardly felt herself sway. It was only when she felt Jace's strong arms around her did Tammy realise, to her chagrin, that she had been suddenly hit by a wave of nausea. Enough to cloud her vision and produce the sickly feeling of vomit present in her stomach.

'Tammy, are you alright?' Jace's face was a picture of worry and his eyes were filled with genuine concern.

'Yes - I think,' She allowed him to steer her to her chair.

'Drink your coffee,' he urged softly.

Tammy did as she was ordered and took a long sip of the warm milky coffee, grateful that the dizzying rush of heat that had followed her nausea was now beginning to subside. She exerted a shallow breath of air to calm herself and then turned and faced Jace with the assurance that she was fine. 'I'm okay.' To her surprise, her voice was muffled and held little conviction.

Jace gently took hold of her free hand and sandwiched it between his own. 'Are you sure?'

His question seemed more probing than taken at face

value, causing Tammy to hesitate, the embarrassment over the entire incident providing the sudden flush to her cheeks. 'Yes, I'm sure,' she stuttered. 'I was just a little shaken.'

Jace leaned forward, close enough so that she was vibrantly aware of the brush of his brows against her forehead. 'You gave me quite a start,' he whispered, his brown eyes watchful as though he preferred to check over her physical stability himself. 'Maybe you should go home.'

'And give you the satisfaction of ending this discussion,' Tammy jabbed poignantly, 'oh no. I want to make it clear right now that I am not going to marry you.'

'Mr Washington!' A doctor, clad hygienically in white, approached the reception area and casually surveyed the small enclosure with a professional eye.

Tammy felt her heart lurch forward sickly as she watched with agonising apprehension the doctor's fast progress toward them. His voice had immediately jerked their prompt attention, causing a myriad of thoughts to instantly run wild through her mind.

Was he bringing bad news; had her grandmother's condition deteriorated; would she be able to see her? He'd asked for Jace. Did that mean he'd already considered her too weak to swallow her grandmother's prognosis?

It occurred to her that Jace had sensed her fear, for his hand had crept up her back to her neck, burrowing beneath her hair to stroke the tension from the overstrained muscles there. Tammy was conscious of the warmth that spread through her body, spurned by the slow kneading of Jace's hand and found that she had derived some small comfort from it.

'I'm Doctor Thompson,' the middle aged man introduced, taking the chair next to Jace. 'We've managed to stabilize your grandmother's condition and she should sleep comfortably through the night.'

'She's my godmother,' Jace clarified, his voice holding the sudden relief that had washed over him. 'She's Tammy's grandmother.'

'I beg your pardon,' the doctor apologised, diverting his attention toward Tammy. 'Perhaps you could tell me precisely what happened?'

Tammy's own relief was suddenly eclipsed with a strange kind of trepidation which she recognised to be nothing more than guilt, shame and a degree of immaturity. If she had had the courage to explain to Hattie exactly what was going on, she wouldn't be sitting there presently, totally fearful of explaining to an upstanding doctor her misguided shortcomings, particularly the one which had led to her grandmother's latest spell.

Knowing of the humiliation she would suffer, Jace immediately interjected, 'I found her.' He saw Tammy's eyebrows lift and her face flush guiltily, but he went on. 'She was lying, collapsed, at the bottom of the stairs. We were hoping you could tell us what happened.'

'It's difficult to ascertain the cause,' the doctor explained. 'I gathered from her hospital notes that she was perfectly well to be discharged. It's puzzling, but in simple terms, she fainted. That's all.'

'Is - is she okay?' Tammy queried, silently thankful of Jace's act of chivalry. She briefly wondered why he did it and stoically decided that it was perhaps in guilt that he too was also to blame.

'She's fine,' she heard the doctor assure gently, 'but we'd like to keep her under observation for a few days, just to be sure.'

'Can I see her?' Tammy asked hesitantly. She knew she owed Hattie an explanation, perhaps several, and wondered what possible compunction she could invent that would sound plausible enough to withstand her grandmother's interrogation.

'Actually,' the doctor declared curiously. 'She asked to see Mr Washington. That's why I thought . . .' He finished the sentence with his eyes, his professional instinct detecting that her grandmother's request was most definitely unusual

Humiliation instantly shadowed Tammy's cheeks. *She* was Mama Hattie's grandaughter. A Caswell. But it was Jace who Hattie wanted to see; Jace who she'd placed her trust and probably her very life.

'You'd better go to her,' Tammy found herself saying, desperately forcing back the bitter tears. 'I'll wait here.'

She knew Jace had been watching her the entire time and sensed that he knew of her pain and anguished shame. When he rose from his chair and placed a comforting hand on her shoulder, Tammy felt the overwhelming urge to burst out into tears, to tell Jace how sorry she was that she'd ever behaved so foolishly, that she should never have argued with him and that his good intentions were precisely that; doing the best for everyone, including herself.

She was glad of the five minutes respite spent alone in Jace's absence to gather her bearings and dry away the tears that had succeeded to tumble down her cheeks. Her grandmother could've died, she thought frightfully, now admitting to the truth. Perhaps she should marry Jace then maybe her life would be less problematic.

After all, she loved him, the company directors wanted him and her grandmother's faith in him were enough reasons to convince and prove that to be the correct decision; but could she live with his hate instead of his love for her?

'A cent for your thoughts.'

Tammy's head shot up dumbfounded and settled on the very features of the man pictured vividly in her mind. She couldn't speak for the shock of finding Jace within her reach when just a few moments ago he was in her head, an image impossible to touch.

'A cruzeiro then,' Jace's voice teased.

'I was just thinking,' she told him slowly, swallowing the

desire that had, with incredible speed, built up inside her.

'Hattie seems to be fine,' Jace assured softly.

Tammy swallowed her breath. 'What - what did she want?'

'I'll tell you outside,' Jace answered. 'Come on.'

THEY WERE in Jace's car, on the journey back to Tammy's apartment, as she'd requested. Jace hadn't yet raised the subject about her grandmother and Tammy wondered nervously whether she should again bring up the topic, but as she looked at him, it became clear to her that he was thinking; seriously thinking. Deciding against breaking his chain of thought, she instead leaned into the soft leather seat and watched as the early morning traffic passed by.

When the car at last came to a halt outside her apartment building, Tammy felt her body stiffen. She was afraid of what Jace would say and warily focussed on her hands in an attempt to avoid his face. She heard him unfasten his seat belt and then release the catch on her own so that the harness sprung loosely up and over her shoulder.

'Comfortable?' his voice asked a second later.

Tammy nodded her head then risked looking at him. The exhaustion of flying back to England and then making the unexpected trip to the hospital had obviously taken its toll. Jace appeared tired and worn out, his face showing that he was evidently in need of some rest. She found herself wanting to place her hand against his cheek, to smooth away the racks that betrayed his fatigue, but instantly squashed the urge, recalling the way he'd treated her earlier.

'This seems as good a place as any to talk,' Jace began heavily, easing into his seat. 'It seems that you'd mistakenly underestimated your grandmother.'

Tammy's face grew alarmed. 'What do you mean?'

'She's always known how Jason feels about you,' Jace

declared sternly.   'But what she wanted to know was whether it was true that you'd left me for him.'

Tammy's voice was tinged with a note of apprehension. 'What - what did you tell her?'

'I told her it wasn't true of course,' Jace said flatly. 'I didn't like the way she placed her hand against her heart, so I also told her that I - we had brought the wedding date forward to this Saturday.'

Tammy sighed. 'What did she say?'

'Naturally, she was delighted,' Jace said firmly. When he didn't hear Tammy's immediate remark in response, he turned and faced her. She was staring as though into space, her expression haunting, fragile, sad even.

In truth, Tammy had never felt so confused in her entire life. On the one hand, she was tormented with memories of tenderness, images of sharing a life together, of having children and of building a relationship that was a union of love and commitment. Yet on the other hand, she knew she wouldn't be wholeheartedly happy living a life that only involved their sexual intimacy and no emotional bonding to speak of, except the written bonding of their marriage certificate of course.

Sherelle's words suddenly ran through her mind. *'Marry the man today and change his ways tomorrow.'* Maybe that was what she should do, Tammy decided suddenly. Maybe in time and given the right homely environment and loving persuasion, Jace would grow to love her too.

'This does make for a very pleasant surprise not to find you objecting,' Jace teased harshly, frazzled by her silence.

'I'm past making my objections,' Tammy tossed, too fed up to fight. 'Just tell me what time I'm expected to be married?'

Jace's brows rose in amazement. 'Ten o'clock.'

'I'll be there.'

CHAPTER ELEVEN

AS JACE watched Tammy walk away toward her apartment, he felt a strange and powerfully familiar emotion budding deep inside him. He'd experienced it several times before where she was concerned, but this time it was stronger, more apparent. It was a combination of tenderness and gentleness, with the added mixture of desire and sensuality that made him feel vulnerable.

In the time he'd known Tammy, she'd amused him, infuriated him past reason and had sexually aroused him to the brink of such exquisite delight, it had been a shock to his entire nervous system.

He'd wanted the ultimate ecstasy, to make love to her, but his emotions had been so exhilarated with the new and unexpected passion he'd felt, that he hadn't realised what he was saying until it was too late.

His conscience pricked him as he recalled the mockery he'd made of her virginity. She'd been so innocent and yet she had had the courage to blatantly defy him and the sheer cunningness to scheme against the pressure he was putting on her.

And he had pressured her. He'd backed her into corners, had stripped her of any options, except the one to marry him, and he was totally disgusted with himself for it. Yet he couldn't stop.

That morning, he'd played on her grandmother's weakness, shamelessly using Hattie's condition as an added excuse to force her into marriage. He was filled with self-loathing over his action, as of the fact that he'd intended to use their marriage as a convenient tool to defend his ego and pride.

Icy regret shot through him. He wished he hadn't behaved so cold-hearted, but he hadn't been able to control himself. From the moment he saw the picture of her and Jason Lee in the newspapers, his mind had conjured up such tormenting pictures of Tammy lying naked in Jason's arms that he found himself taking desperate measures. He had told himself he would rather she was subjugated to him than have her belong to anyone else.

Jace leaned into his car seat, confused. He should have stuck to their original agreement. They were only to fabricate a romance until her grandmother was well enough to be discharged from the hospital; their marriage only to be a last resort if that tactic was forced to come into play. That was the plan.

He would have stuck to is too had he not seen Tammy looking so glamorous and sexy at the charity gala. Damned that provocative red dress, Jace cursed, the sudden thought of her in it stirring a hardness within him that instantly tightened his loins.

The effect she had on him was incredible, he mused, adjusting his position. Perhaps the same effect she had on Jason Lee. How could she have kissed that jerk? an inner voice raged. Jealously ripped through Jace like a wild fury, slashing at his emotions until it cut through to his heart.

She'd denied ever going to bed with Jason and had told him that the kiss had been given at Christmas, at a time when he knew spirits to be high and mistletoe to be present. God knows he'd kissed many a women himself under similar circumstances, so why hadn't he believed her?

Maybe he wanted to punish her for allowing Jason near her, or maybe it was because she hadn't made love to him. Maybe, Jace decided, it was because he knew deep down that she hated him and had only agreed to the marriage out of shame and more precisely, for his money. She'd wanted three million and he'd offered to give it to her. Hell, he didn't know why, nor could he understand why on earth he was forcing Tammy to marry him. He should be running as far away from her as he could, a choice his personal accountant would have advised.

That unwanted emotion stirred within him again, but Jace instantly cast it aside. All he knew was that he wanted Tammy because she was a beautiful enigma and because he didn't want her to end up between the sheets of an insipid jackass like Jason Lee who probably made love fumbling in the dark. He wanted her because he desired her more than anything he'd ever wanted and because . . . because, more often than not, he always got what he wanted. That was why. Nothing more.

TAMMY STEPPED nervously from the en suite shower cubicle and padded with wet feet toward her bedroom, promptly reminding herself that it was Saturday, her wedding day.

She felt a sudden urge to pinch herself and infact did so, just to be certain that she was awake and that the entire drama which had led to that day had not been some imaginary figmentation of her mind. But the pinch left its tell tale mark, proving beyond doubt that everything had been a definite reality and not some wild dream or fantasy.

Inhaling a slow ragged breath, she placed a dry towel around her dripping hair and sat down on her bed, reflecting on how chaotic the day before had been.

Friday was full of chaos. The telephone hadn't stopped ringing and the press took it upon themselves to beseige and bombard her with photographers and reporters who'd followed her every movement to and from her apartment.

They'd wanted to know why Jason Lee had been fired, which was news to her, and why they had been misled with information they'd claimed had been provided via a reliable source. Her only thoughts then were bemusement over how the wedding details had been leaked and the inner reserve to quickly conclude her shopping and return home before their questions succeeded in upsetting her.

She'd taken a trip to Harrods, for a short time escaping the scrutiny of the presshounds, as she bought herself an ivory suit with co-ordinating hat, gloves and shoes, recalling that she hadn't anything suitable in her extensive wardrobe. She had been internally relieved when she was at last able to shut out the world on returning to her apartment.

If she'd kept her old flamboyant id, she would have had an outrageous bridal shower party in the Caswell tradition Jace so openly despised, Tammy told herself with a grin, probably with a selection of the bared tawny biceps of the *Satisfaction* posse for good measure to really liven things up.

The smile creased along her cheeks as she recalled how much she used to love the night pace, enjoying life to the fullest because it had been expected of her and because she was a Caswell. But after the ceremony that morning, she would be Tammy Lola Washington and she would be expected to live up to the Washington tradition, whatever that was.

Tammy patted the wetness from her hair and suddenly thought, something old, something new, something borrowed and something blue. She would wear her mother's earrings, she decided, applying pressure to the towel, and the new brooch in her jewellery box which she'd never worn, but she hadn't anything blue and there was no one with her from whom she could borrow something. Oh bother, she hissed to herself, tossing the towel aside to slip into her cream lacy underwear. It was all nonsense anyway.

She walked over to her bedroom window and momentarily glanced through the net Austrian curtaining. For 8.30 in the morning, the sky was remarkably clear and it seemed the sun would probably raise its lazy head to brighten up the day.

At least she knew now it wasn't going to rain and

Tammy felt silently thankful that the weather wasn't going to pose any threat by dampening her mood. Not that she felt anything would, but she so desperately wanted everything to be just as she'd imagined it; the ceremony an intimate and private affair, Jace afterward holding her in his arms and telling her how much he loved her ...

An hour later, Tammy was fully dressed, feeling calm and confident and certain about what she was doing. With a positive mind about her future, she smoothed the soft line in her skirt and took a glimpse of herself in the wardrobe mirror. Instantly, a rope of tension coiled its way around her chest, suffocating her to the point that she was forced to sit down for fear of fainting. Until that moment, she'd felt perfectly fine, but now, seeing how fresh and vibrant she appeared, an ambivalent thought caused Tammy to question her own mind.

She shouldn't be getting married like this, totally alone and alienated, with her hands tied and her only reasons, aside from love, being on the strength of her grandmother's weakness, Jace's emotional blackmail and pressure from the paparazzi.

It was shame over Hattie's condition which had led her to yield to Jace's demand in the first place; shame, guilt and the knowledge that he had good intentions. She knew she would be well provided for financially and that Jace would expect her to be a dutiful wife in every respect, but again Tammy questioned whether that would be enough. Surely love had to count too.

Suddenly the doorbell peeled loudly into her thoughts. Curious as to who it could be, Tammy left her bedroom and opened the Regency door. 'Calvin, what are you doing here?' she said startled, watching as her brother, fully dressed for the occasion, walked boldy into the entrance hall.

'I'm taking you to the registry office,' Calvin smiled warmly. 'I'm the come-best-man, come-give-away-bride stand in, if there is such a thing for a registry wedding.'

'There isn't,' Tammy affirmed, deducting that he had obviously spoken to Jace, 'but I guess there are no prizes for who you've been talking to.'

'Now come on sis,' Calvin scowled. 'You can't blame me for seeing the merits in being related to the boss. As brother-in-law, I should imagine my business life to be quite cosy at the office. No more marketing migraine, advertising allergy, dyspeptic bottle design, media melancholia or art ache.'

'Funny,' Tammy chided recklessly. 'I thought the executive vice president's job carried a capacity of responsibility, for someone that is, who doesn't mind catching a little work wart. Suffering the usual creative cosmetic claustrophobia Calvin, or is it just idle insomnia?'

Calvin stepped back in surprise. 'You know about the new job?'

'Why else would you be here,' Tammy retorted.

'Well, this is family business,' Calvin said a little shamefaced.

'And since when have you been so family minded?'

'Sis I . . .'

'Hello Tammy.' Calvin was blessedly saved the humiliation of explaining as Sherelle Tate stepped into the hallway, immaculately dressed in lilac and co-ordinating accessories. 'I hope you don't mind me being here,' she said with excitement, 'but I can't resist weddings.'

She handed Tammy a bouquet of white and yellow flowers. 'I bought you these, then I remembered something else and had to run back to the car for it.' She cheekily held up a blue garter.

Tammy chuckled back her tears. 'You shouldn't have done this for me.' She hadn't even thought of flowers, let alone a garter.

'Now sis, no tears,' Calvin ordered, lending her his handkerchief. 'We're expected at the registry in less than half an hour.'

Tammy immediately panicked. 'I don't know why I'm doing this. He doesn't even love me.'

'But you love him don't you?' Sherelle probed.

'Yes I do.'

'Then put your garter on girl and let's get going.'

Tammy leaned against the plush cream leather in the back seat of Calvin's Mercedes, clutching at the flowers, her body nervous, tense and afraid. This was the day she had looked forward to all her life. Infact, as a child growing up, she had all the classic daydreams of a husband, children and the kind of domestic happiness that would complete such a family unit.

Then her young adult life went one further with all the fashionable dreams of love, passion and that special something that would fill the empty yearning she had inside. So why did she feel so shell shocked? Was it the fact that she had come to accept reality and the cruel realisation that Jace may never love her?

Tammy gnawed anxiously at her bottom lip, telling herself that if there was an iota of truth in that, then neither she or Jace would be committing themselves to that terrifying fate.

He wanted her sexually, she knew that and he'd told her that he cared about her. Jace had even called her at some unearthly hour in the morning, by her own standards, to tell her he couldn't get her out of his mind. And when he kissed her, it was like the world had disappeared, nothing existing except the eager yearning and anticipated pleasure they had for one another. Quite apart from the circumstances which had led to that day, Tammy badly wanted to marry Jace, as much as she wanted him to love her.

'I suppose you've heard about Jason Lee,' Calvin said casually as he turned a bend. 'I've known that man eight years, but I'd never have thought he could stoop so low. He'd really excelled himself.'

Tammy's attention was instantly propelled from her

chain of thoughts. 'What - what happened?'

'He was a one man crusade on a smear campaign targeted at Jace,' Calvin explained. 'I guess I'm in part to blame for my contingency plan B by putting the idea into his head about tipping the press, but he played havoc disclosing information that was totally disreputable to the company by speaking out personally against Jace. The man's the damn chairman for heaven's sake.'

'You've changed your tune,' Tammy said wide eyed. 'I thought *you'd* played a hand in that.'

'*Me!*' Calvin squealed. 'I wouldn't do anything that extreme. All I said to the press was that my sister was enjoying the avid attentions of an old admirer who wanted to marry her. I had a time telling Jace that last night. I thought maybe he'd punch me out again.'

'Did he?'

'No,' Calvin said with expressed relief. 'Though I deserved it. And listen sis,' he added, taking another bend. 'I know now how selfish I've been, treating you the way I have and not going to see grandmother. After the wedding, I'm going to go and straighten things out with her.'

Tammy's mouth fell open. It was unlike Calvin to show any molecule of consideration, perhaps as much as it was unlike Jason to have been so malicious and spiteful.

'Here we are,' Calvin said cheerfully fifteen minutes later. 'Westminster Registry Office.'

'What have you done to Calvin?' Tammy whispered to Sherelle by way of deflecting her nerves as she stepped from the car. 'I hardly know him today.'

'I knocked some sense into him,' Sherelle laughed as she gently urged Tammy toward the entrance door.

Tammy froze the instant they preceded Calvin into the building. Somewhere in there, Jace was waiting for her, she thought frantically.

'Relax,' Sherelle whispered, sensing her tension. 'It'll be over soon.'

Will it? Tammy rationalised that thought to herself.

What about *after* the wedding? Cautiously, her gaze strayed across the waiting room, past the flight of empty chairs and landed on the small party across from her. The compelling brown eyes that met hers were soft and warm, and sensually inviting as they appraised every delicate curve of her body.

Tammy's heart fluttered against her ribcage as her gaze took in Jace's handsome features and the elegant ease with which he wore his grey suit, impeccably tailored to fit his tall, muscular frame. She noticed every familiar thing about him, from the shadow of his moustache to the mass of thick dark hair freshly groomed for the occasion. Then she spotted the three people by his side, his parents; their very presence adding to her heightened tension, and a younger woman who she assumed to be none other than Jace's adopted sister.

'You're late,' Jace said quietly, having obliterated the short distance between. 'I thought maybe you weren't coming.'

'It's the bride's prerogative to be late,' Tammy whispered curtly, the tension evident in her voice as she turned an expectant gaze toward his sister.

She had wanted him to comment on how she looked, or to have said something nice, even though she was fully aware by the way Jace stood over her in an imposing manner, his eyes appreciating her fresh, enticingly attractive appearance, that he was obviously affected by her.

Nevertheless, Tammy thought absurdly, her nerves would have benefitted from the boisterous tonic of a verbal compliment, even if Jace felt she didn't deserve to be flattered. 'This must be Marchi,' she added politely, thankful of the sudden control her voice ejected.

'Hello,' the petite woman smiled warmly, amusement dancing in her brown eyes as she added, 'Ignore Jace, he's a little edgy.'

Tammy nervously sliced her gaze toward Jace who

hadn't taken his eyes of her. 'They're waiting for us,' he exclaimed, his expression guarded as he reached out to gently take her arm. 'In ten minutes, we'll be married.'

Her brows rose in sudden speculation. *In ten minutes we'll be married.* Jace's words repeated in her head gave Tammy the impression that he had given her a choice - freedom to change her mind, or a life in marriage to him.

She wondered why he chose to add a tone of caution now, moments before they were due to say their vows. Did he really think she would still refuse him like she'd promised aeons ago? For that was how long it seemed to Tammy from the day she'd first tossed out her reluctance by telling Jace that her absence would appropriately be at the altar.

She'd never expected to come this far, yet here she was, waiting to marry the man she once despised, the man who had once been a threat to the company and to Calvin's inheritance. She gazed with loving eyes at his tall, indomitable frame, her mind registering the subtle power etched into every masculine feature of his proud face.

He had won it all, control of the company, chairmanship of the Board and more precisely, he'd won her. It seemed the most natural thing in the world to yield to the strain he'd put on her, to follow her heart in spite of everything, because contrary to her earlier defiance of him, she was going to go all the way.

Tipping her head as though to assert the point, Tammy said a little headstrong, 'Let's not keep them waiting.'

'BY THE authority vested in me, I now pronounce you husband and wife. You may kiss the bride.'

Tammy felt her heart somersault as the registrar's words bellowed softly into her head. She was married, bonded in matrimony to the man she loved.

In her state of euphoria, she was aware of Jace's sudden closeness, of his head coming within inches of her own. His hands slid up her arm to gently imprison her shoulders, and in helpless anticipation, she watched his soft, inviting lips slowly descend to hers.

Their mouths met in a heated kiss that was eagerly insistent and yet gently coaxing. Tammy arched herself eagerly toward Jace, not in humble suplication, but in proud demand, knowing that whatever the differences were between them, they were united in wedlock and perhaps one day, she hoped, in love. For she was no longer Jace's significant other, no longer someone with whom he could assimilate a romance, but his wife, his new bride.

As her lips held him closer, savouring his passionate assault, Tammy's mind told her that Jace now had rights to her affections and more appropriately, to her body. Tonight, he had the right to take her in his arms, to join his body with hers and to arouse and caress her until she submitted to the demands of his maleness.

An unfamiliar eagerness to reach out to him and show Jace with her lips just what delight it gave her to have him near her suddenly overwhelmed Tammy. Tonight, she would give herself to him with all the love and passion she'd kept locked inside for so long. And tonight, Tammy decided with a heady new feeling of pleasure and ardent joy at the sensation of Jace's tongue pulsing softly against her lips, she would tell him how much she loved him.

'Ehey, we're still here you know,' Calvin's chuckling voice intruded into the bliss of their moment, promptly reminding Tammy exactly where she was.

She pulled back into Jace's arms, sensing his relunctance as she watched him throw an annoyed look across the small group, his face irritable as though their very presence constituted a personal threat to him.

'I think we have to sign something,' she whispered a little embarrassed, turning expectantly toward the registrar.

Ten minutes later, they were in the BMW driving home, having said their goodbyes to Jace's family and obliging Calvin with a few polaroid snapshots to take to Hattie at the hospital, and the waiting photographers who had their press deadlines to meet.

Someone, Tammy considered to be none other than Calvin himself, had tied balloons to the car rear, aptly inscribed with the words *'just married'* for everyone to see.

A smile creased her lips as she leaned comfortably against the passenger seat, happy and sated, her mind silently reflecting on the day and the ceremony which had been for her, a private and special occasion.

Jace's father had produced the exquisite diamond studded gold band which was now sitting prettily against the diamond solitaire on her left hand and Calvin, to her surprise, the initialed gold ring which she'd placed on Jace's ring finger as a token of her love.

She was later to learn from Calvin that Jace had selected the rings himself the day before, expressing his heartfelt belief that they both should wear one.

Her heart warmed as she turned to face his watchful expression, uncomprehending the change in him from that of the immoral lover she'd once accused him of, to the now devoted, upstanding married man. This was the man she'd yearned for, she mused, watching as he took the bend toward Kensington, the man she'd waited for all her life.

She contemplated that he was taking her home to pack a suitcase preparatory to announcing that they would be flying to some place of seclusion for their honeymoon. Her smile deepened as she considered how she should react. Surprised, or calmly indifferent? Deep down Tammy knew she would be estatic wherever Jace was taking her.

She would pack her yellow bikini, she calculated, already surmising that they were visiting some warm climate in the Caribbean, and her camera, she suddenly reckoned, thrilled with the prospect of taking pictures of their first intimate time together.

When the car finally pulled to a stop outside her apartment, Tammy had already added five other things to her mental list of luggage, and was lamely suppressing the excitement that was bursting inside her. This was it, Jace was going to announce their honeymoon destination.

She eagerly turned to face him, her heart quickening in anticipation of the news, but nothing could have prepared her more for the blow Jace's words were to inflict.

'I'll see you when I get back from Brazil,' he announced calmly, releasing her seatbelt in the process. 'Give Hattie my regards.'

Tammy's eyes immediately widened in alarmed amazement. 'What - what are you talking about?'

'I'm flying back to Brazil tonight,' Jace repeated, flicking open the car door. 'I'm sure you'll manage without me for a week.'

Tammy watched with disbelief as Jace stepped from the car, swallowing the hardened lump in her throat that suddenly seemed to be lodged there as her mind spun in perplexity and sheer amazement.

He couldn't be serious, her mind screamed, not at a time like this, not on their wedding day. But as she turned and watched Jace through the rear window stoop to release the balloons from the car bumber, some inner logic warned her that he wasn't joking at all.

She felt herself move from the car seat, and yet Tammy was not really conscious that she'd left it until she found herself stood next to Jace at the boot of the car, her mind thinking, wondering what she should say to rationalise the situation.

She took a full minute to pull herself together before she asked, 'Why are you going?'

'Because I have work to do,' Jace answered without looking at her.

'Well why now?' Tammy insisted, her alarm brinking on panic, 'after you've gone to the trouble of marrying me?'

Jace kept his head dipped and released the last of the balloons before he turned to Tammy, his expression impassive. 'I married you in honour of our agreement.'

'Don't prevaricate the truth to me,' Tammy felt her fury begin to simmer. She could sense that, as well as being angry with her, Jace was furious with himself for something, and yet there was also another dimension to his attitude that she couldn't quite fathom, but she felt certain they all led to one thing. 'This isn't about my grandmother because she's fine,' she said recklessly, 'and it isn't about our agreement because I was always relunctant to agree to anything. This is about me and Jason Lee isn't it?'

Grasping her arm, Jace turned her forcibly to face him. 'What else has he taken that rightly belongs to me?' he countered treacherously. 'I want to know.'

'Nothing!' Tammy insisted, knowing from his shadowed brown eyes that Jace wasn't at all convinced. 'But you can believe what you like. Believe that I'm play acting again if that makes you happy. I'm beside justifying myself.' She swallowed her bitterness before adding, 'I should imagine after our annulment that I'll find someone who really deserves me.'

'I won't agree to an annulment,' Jace said flatly, tightening his grip on her arm.

'Then it'll have to be a decree absolute by divorce,' Tammy admonished madly, jerking her arm to release herself. 'I'll not live my life in a loveless marriage to you.'

She felt herself shiver as she turned and began a quick pursuit toward her apartment, though the slight vibration was not from cold. It was from her sheer stupidity and idiotic fantasy of ever thinking that she could actually change Jace Washington, that she could ever make him love her.

Already the acrimony inside her had built to a point that she could literally taste the bitterness on her tongue. Jace hated her and he was punishing her and she loathed his very treatment.

Tammy didn't hear his footsteps behind her until she felt the pressure of Jace's hand on her shoulder. 'What about everything I've done for you, you ungrateful little tease,' Jace fired sharply. 'If it wasn't for my quick thinking, Dr Thompson would've learned the real truth behind your grandmother's latest spell.'

'In my book, that was all your fault,' Tammy gasped in annoyance that he would still blame her entirely. 'And all you've proved is that chivalry isn't dead.'

'You're not without blame,' Jace bellowed. 'If you hadn't kissed Jason Lee . . .'

'We're back to that again,' Tammy interrupted with grit. 'How absurd. Why don't you just satisfy yourself and accuse me of dramatising the kiss I gave you this morning, then you needn't worry about whether the one I gave Jason two years ago was real or not.'

'Was it?' Jace stepped back, charting her expression carefully. He hated himself for what he was thinking, for his stupid jealousy and the way he was feeling about her, but if only she would show him some sign that she could genuinely care for him, perhaps one day love him, then he would be prepared to believe and forgive her anything.

Instead, Tammy backed a cautious step out of his reach, her eyes blazing with hurt and contempt as she lied gravely. 'Yes it was real. It happened a long time ago, but like you, I remember it as though it'd happened yesterday and I enjoyed it. Satisfied now?'

Jace felt his jealousy mount to such an intensity, he hardly knew how to cope with it. He felt destroyed, bruised, pain even and yet his pride refused to let go. He would exact his revenge by taking her to his bed and drown her in a pool of ecstasy until she forget that there ever existed a man named Jason Lee. He would teach her to please him too. He would *make* her love him. 'I'll be satisfied in a hour from now,' he told her tersely. 'Ideally, I would've liked to have whisked you off to a honeymoon suite somewhere, but under the circumstances, your bedroom will do.'

Tammy retreated two steps in panic, but pretentiously inflated her bravado. 'Tossing back your own words, *my* co-operation isn't a pre-requisite to this marriage either.'

'It is now,' Jace declared, advancing two steps toward her. 'I told you once that I'd do my damest to consummate our marriage if we got this far and I intend to do precisely that, although I would rather hope to have your co-operation. Your *active* co-operation.'

'All you would prove is that you can overpower me,' Tammy said nervously, edging toward the main entrance door of her apartment building, 'and - and that you could carry me off by force.'

Caught with her back against the doors, she stood paralysed as Jace came up and caged her firmly in his arms. Suddenly, the demanding heat of his body sent piercing stabs of desire to shoot throughout her entire nervous system, triggering a spasm of passion that began to simmer in Tammy's guts as Jace locked her fiercely against his chest.

Then his head dipped and Tammy felt her lips captured in a ravenous, bruising kiss that was filled with a raw, insistent urgency she felt powerless to resist, though her first reaction had been to fight Jace off.

Some inner instinct told her that he had intended to savagely kiss her, but the instant his mouth parted against her lips, his kiss gentled to a slow, melting hunger which deepened moment by moment, that a shower of fiery darts of excitement immediately coarsed the length of her body.

She heard her name whispered softly against her lips seconds before Jace explored the delicate contours of her mouth, tasting and shaping the sensitive flesh there before his tongue delved and claimed the hot, fevered need that was the very heat of her breath. Then, without warning, Jace was releasing her, pulling her arms away from his shoulders as though she had hurt him in someway.

Tammy could see the passion in his eyes as he gazed at her, but Jace's voice was icy cold when he spoke. 'I know what I said just now, but I'm into seduction not rape,' he told her flatly. 'And as much as I want you, I'll not force you against your will, especially at the risk of you pretending to enjoy it.'

Before Tammy could even grasp the essence of her feelings, or even come to terms with the sudden loss of the source that had incited them, Jace was already striding back to his car. Within seconds, he was gone, leaving her bereft, aroused and shaking with a combination of emotions, one of which she unwantedly identified. Regret.

CHAPTER TWELVE

THE TAXI pulled up on Park Lane outside the London Hilton and Tammy promptly paid the driver before she stepped nervously from the car.

Slightly giddy from the whisky she'd taken two hours earlier to numb the pain, hurt and misery Jace had caused her, she plucked up her courage and entered the hotel reception.

It took all her confidence and the production of her marriage certificate to convince the hotel attendant who she was in order to be given an entry key to the Deluxe suite. The room had apparently been booked in the names of Mr & Mrs Washington so she was able to fabricate an excuse as to why she was arriving there alone. As she ascended in the elevator with the hotel porter, Tammy suddenly felt grateful for having taken three measures of whisky as her nerves were now aptly controlled to confront Jace head on.

She'd been more than a little surprised on calling his penthouse with the pretext of an apology, to learn from an equally surprised Marchi that Jace had booked into the five star hotel and was not scheduled to fly back to Brazil until the following month. She'd replaced the receiver and immediately called a taxi, determined that she would find out why he'd lied to her.

Yet the moment she left the elevator car and followed the hotel porter toward her room, Tammy felt her hands tremor with renewned apprehension and wished she'd taken a fourth measure of scotch if only for stamina.

Finally, they reached the door and the hotel porter

inserted the key into the lock. After tipping him, Tammy closed the door and looked around. The suite at first seemed empty on her approach and for a fleeting moment, Tammy wondered whether Jace had come there at all.

Then as she deposited her handbag on a nearby table, she heard the sound of running water and followed the faint, trickling noise until it took her through a wide dimly lit lounge, past a mini bar and into a larger, elegantly furnished bedroom where everything from the curtains to the bed covers co-ordinated in floral shades of peach, green and yellow.

Tammy's hazel gaze swept quickly across the room's interior, taking in the bucket of champagne and the delightful complimentary flowers perched on a table stationed near glass doors which she noticed led to a balcony overlooking Hyde Park. Then she suddenly caught herself up short when Jace unexpectedly walked out of an en suite bathroom she hadn't realised was adjoining the bedroom, totally unclothed as the day he was born.

His deep brown eyes narrowed in on her without flinching, his chiseled features a mask of stone as he watched her silently take in with fascinated interest his wet, virile cinnamon brown body.

'How did you know that I was here?' he asked coldly, slowly reaching for a white towel on the bed which he proceeded without haste to wrap loosely around his handsome torso.

Tammy swallowd her breath. 'I called your home.' When Jace didn't respond, she added, 'And apparently you're not scheduled to return to Brazil until next month.'

Jace padded with wet feet toward a button control embedded into a wall panel. 'Would it have made any difference?' he asked, adjusting the air conditioning.

Tammy stared at him in genuine puzzlement, his hard muscular chest attracting her attention. 'Difference to what?' she queried.

'Our honeymoon.'

12.   Do you consider yourself to be a . . .
        (you may select no more than two)

a   ▢   Professional woman
b   ▢   Homemaker
c   ▢   Careergirl
d   ▢   Mother
e   ▢   Student
f   ▢   Other (specify) ....

13.   Is fashion important to you?

a   ▢   Yes
b   ▢   No
c   ▢   Not bothered

14.   What did you like about this Peacock Novel?
        (you may select more than one)

a   ▢   Front cover art.
b   ▢   The Afro lifestyle incorporated into the story.
c   ▢   The opportunity to purchase other products.
d   ▢   Everything including other aspects not listed.
e   ▢   My letter/further comments are attached.

15.   How much do you earn per annum?

a   ▢   Under £10,000/$20,000
b   ▢   £10,000-£15,000/$20,00-$35,000
c   ▢   £15,000-£20,000/$35,000-$45,000
c   ▢   More

16.   Would you like to be put on our mailing list to be updated
        on our latest publications?

a   ▢   No
b   ▢   Yes   My name and address is detailed below.

NAME _____

ADDRESS_____

_____

ZIP/POST CODE _____

Send to: COUNTRY _____

        Peacock Publishing Media MX1* P.O. Box 438
        Sheffield S1 4YX ENGLAND

If ordering AFRODERMA product, keep entire questionnaire and order form intact. Return to AFRODERMA Department at address given below.

Cut --

AFRODERMA ORDER FORM

Please send me my free Tondo with the following order. One gift per customer. Please state quantity. Completion and return of Peacock Novel questionnaire with this order qualifies a £3.00 discount off <u>one</u> AFRODERMA Ablution Wash to £8.95.

.... AFRODERMA Ablution Wash. 100 ml £11.95
.... AFRODERMA Tondo £2.95 (FREE with this order)

PAYMENT DETAILS

Please enclose a remittance to the value of the product/s ordered, adding £1.00 (outside UK add £1.50) to cover postage and packing, regardless of quantity.

Payment may be made in sterling by UK personal cheque, postal order, or sterling international money order made payable to The Peacock Company.

Please complete in BLOCK CAPITALS

NAME _____

ADDRESS _____

CITY/TOWN _____

COUNTY/STATE _____

POST/ZIP CODE _____ COUNTRY _____

TELEPHONE NO _____

Please allow up to 28 days for delivery.

Send to:

AFRODERMA Department, The Peacock Company,
P O Box 438 SHEFFIELD S1 4YX ENGLAND